'Poor little rich boy,' Blythe murmured with mock sympathy.

'Ah, Blythe, I'm beginning to understand why you were picked. Most women melt on the spot and vow to dedicate their lives to making a home for me.'

'You don't have much respect for women, do you?' Blythe followed it with a casually dismissive shrug, her own long lashes screening the anger she felt. 'I'm not sure if I have either, if they're silly enough to take you seriously.'

'A mistake you'll never make,' he said.

IN PURSUIT OF LOVE

BY

JAYNE BAULING

MILLS & BOON LIMITED
ETON HOUSE   18-24 PARADISE ROAD
RICHMOND   SURREY   TW9 1SR

*First published in Great Britain 1991
by Mills & Boon Limited*

© Jayne Bauling 1991

*Australian copyright 1991
Philippine copyright 1992
This edition 1992*

ISBN 0 263 77404 X

*Set in Times Roman 10 on 11½ pt.
01-9201-54834 C*

Made and printed in Great Britain

CHAPTER ONE

THE man was impossible!

Blythe Steed supposed Mr Lau had warned her. What had he said?

'He's a playboy,' he had stated primly, and she had suppressed a smile at the old-fashioned word. 'The last girl who served as his assistant here failed to understand that. There was an incident—I expect you know?'

Blythe did. She had heard the story from her colleagues when she had first joined Triple A, and it had been revived when they had heard that the airline's owner was about to descend on them.

'Yes, sir,' she said.

'His last instruction to me before he left was to find someone...er...someone sophisticated to act as his assistant next time he came to Hong Kong. An irregular request with which I'm complying by taking irregular steps, bypassing Personnel and borrowing you. Can you cope?'

She could have told him he was making a mistake, but she didn't think it was relevant. She had encountered playboys before, although none as internationally notorious as the great Christian Ballantine, and they had left her unimpressed. Why should he be any different?

'I think so, Mr Lau,' she had assured him confidently.

And here she was, having to resist a rare impulse to stamp her foot.

'Mr Ballantine, I am trying to behave professionally, but you aren't exactly making it easy for me.'

Curiously light blue eyes swept her face once more, and the smile accompanying the insolent inspection was cynical.

'I'm sure you're very professional, Blythe.' The deep voice was as warm and lazy as a drowsy caress.

'That just illustrates what I'm saying,' Blythe asserted emphatically. 'Every word you've spoken to me from the moment we were introduced has been along those same offensive lines. If I don't suit you, there are simpler, more courteous ways of getting rid of me. All you had to do was have a quiet word with Mr Lau when we were at the Triple A offices and let him know that you found me utterly impossible.'

But even before he had said a word he had managed to incense her, simply by being the man he was, superbly confident and arrogantly aware of the effect he had on women. Oh, he hadn't done anything as crudely obvious as holding her hand or her eyes too long, but he had definitely done something.

'But I don't know yet that I do find you impossible,' Christian Ballantine returned blandly.

'Obviously there's something wrong with me,' she snapped. 'And with the chauffeur Mr Lau laid on, presumably, since you dismissed him so impatiently.'

They still stood beside the white Rolls-Royce in which they had travelled up to the Peak. Behind them, the graceful, honey-coloured house lovingly imitated the steep rise and fall of the land on which it was built, comprising several levels in order to blend into the landscape, while far below them Hong Kong's rearing skyscrapers were softened to dreaming unreality by the white heat-haze of a late July afternoon.

Only that morning Blythe had paused, entranced by the view, but now she was indifferent to it, her full attention given to the man who surveyed her from a height of six feet.

'I prefer to drive myself. But I'm beginning to think that it's Lau who's got something wrong with him,' he suggested coolly. 'It's his choice that intrigues me and, I'll admit, arouses my suspicions. Does he think I'm a fool? Why you?'

For a moment the heavy sweep of Blythe's eyelids, subtly smudged with shadow just a few shades deeper than her creamy-brown skin, concealed the smoky hazel eyes, but then she flung back her head, her pouting red mouth breaking into the provocative smile that always gave rise to second thoughts in those who had first seen her unsmiling and thought they knew what she was all about.

'Because I'm supposed to be able to cope with you.'

The announcement failed to disconcert him.

'And are you coping?' he asked interestedly.

'I will,' she claimed, defiantly refusing to suspect that Mr Lau might have made a graver miscalculation than the one she was aware of.

'How can you know what it is that you have to cope with?' he derided softly. 'You weren't with Triple A last time I was in Hong Kong, more than a year ago.'

'But the legend lives on,' Blythe offered mockingly.

The dark face tightened fractionally. 'Office gossip.'

'Not necessarily—and not from Mr Lau,' she added loyally. 'But naturally he'd be failing both you as Triple A's owner and his employer, and me as an employee, if he'd omitted to give me some intimation of what to expect, not to mention what might be expected of me.'

'Professionally, of course.'

'There you go again! Of course professionally,' she snapped.

'And how many of your expectations have been confirmed so far?'

'One. I expected you to be difficult, and you are. Oh, it was phrased more tactfully than that. They used words like temperamental, or highly strung.'

'But you call it difficult.' The merest trace of amusement inflected his voice now.

'Impossible was one word that occurred to me. Or spoilt,' Blythe added tartly. 'You are, aren't you? You've got it all, and then some more. Head of Ballantine Holdings, the umbrella for all sorts of enterprises all over the world, homes in London, New York and Hong Kong, thirty years old, successful——'

'Don't forget my brains, my beauty and a fair amount of brawn,' he inserted facetiously.

'I was coming to those. I was about to add intelligence and sex-appeal,' murmured Blythe, having been acutely aware of both from the moment of their meeting. 'Although I've heard that the intelligence is sufficient to isolate you, and I don't personally go for the sort of appeal that relies on so much arrogance.'

But he was undoubtedly a physically attractive man, despite that arrogance stamping the dark face. His elegant lightweight suit somehow emphasised his intense masculinity, and an indolent grace was oddly allied to the impact of his essential vitality and strength. Black-haired and blue-eyed, a combination which had always appealed to her, he was rendered more dangerously attractive than classically handsome by the harsh curve of his nose and the cynicism that shaped his mouth, because the absence of vulnerability or softness implicit in them would challenge any woman. There was too his stark sexuality, the statement he made simply by being, by the way he looked at her, and presumably at all women, his awareness of femininity a proclamation of his own maleness.

'Does it bother you?' he queried.

'I'll get used to it.'

She had to. The frequency with which she had begun to experience a kick of physical reaction had begun to infuriate Blythe, and it was something she had to get under control if he was going to accept her as his personal assistant during the months he planned to spend in Hong Kong, because she knew better than to let herself be interested in a man like Christian Ballantine.

He was saying, 'If by professional you really meant businesslike, why are we tripping over the fringes of the personal?'

'I was under the impression that you had difficulty making the division.'

'As I said, office gossip,' he repeated flatly.

'And the answer to your question, Mr Ballantine,' Blythe said ironically. 'Why me? You may have forgotten, but I gather that it's written in letters of fire in Mr Lau's heart. When you last left Hong Kong, you told him that next time you came you expected him to provide you with someone more sophisticated than the girl who acted as your assistant then.'

'Lord, yes, I remember!' The exclamation was disgusted. 'The stupid little girl decided she was in love with me.'

The droop of her eyelids hid the sparkle of anger in Blythe's eyes as she shook her head in mock incredulity, the fair lights in her mass of soft brown curls dancing in the hazy sunlight.

'How strange of her. Quite inexplicable, wasn't it?' She raised her gaze slowly and met his suspicious look. 'And then had her heart broken when you flaunted your infidelity.'

'You know the story,' he conceded drily, but a glint in the light eyes warned her that she might be about to witness a display of the famous Ballantine temper. 'And on that single incident you, and Lau, and the office gossips, base your knowledge of me, make assumptions about my proclivities...to the extent that I get a houri like you thrown at me!'

'Oh, more than that,' Blythe corrected him smartly, deciding to ignore the personal reference. 'You obviously dislike your reputation, but I understand that it's well earned, and confirming it are all those girls who've been sent out from your other bases to do time in Hong Kong, most of them also nursing broken hearts when they arrive. I've always wondered, though. Is a transfer meant as a reward, or compensation?'

'Neither. Nothing so disinterested.' He paused, giving her a deliberate smile. 'The removals are solely for my benefit.'

'Because they're a reproach to your conscience?' Blythe didn't believe it for a moment and her soft, smokily mocking voice made no secret of her scepticism. 'Or perhaps you're putting temptation out of reach?'

'You know the answer.' In some obscure way, he was challenging her. 'I'm getting them out of my life, out of my hair, as the idiom has it.'

'Your bed,' she suggested.

'Oh, no. You called them girls, and you're so right. I don't take inexperienced, romantic-minded girls who confuse the yearnings of the flesh with the follies of the heart into my bed; nor do I accept invitations to share theirs. So you see, there are no reproaches to my conscience. If they choose to make fools of themselves, without any encouragement, then they have only themselves to blame.'

'And they do choose, of course. Poor Mr Ballantine, it must be hell,' Blythe sympathised sweetly, adding honey to the smoke, although it occurred to her that he was slightly defensive, protesting perhaps just a little too much.

He laughed abruptly, acknowledging the mockery.

'An irritation, anyway. And so, to spare me, Lau has selected you as the member of staff least likely to make a fool of herself. Perhaps I went over the top when I made my future requirements known last time I was here, since it seems that that's exactly what he's done now, but I was under provocation.'

'He'd have loaned you his own assistant, Mrs Keng, except that she's on maternity leave,' Blythe mentioned.

'So I'm landed with you, a sultry, sexy siren——'

'Who will spare you the embarrassment and annoyance of falling in love with you,' she pointed out swiftly. 'Doesn't that advantage compensate for any other deficiencies?'

'Hasn't the man ever heard of a happy medium? As a solution, I find you somewhat extreme. Suppose the reverse of the usual thing happens and I find myself obsessed with you?'

'Except that it seems unlikely, it would be a kind of justice, wouldn't it?' she prompted amusedly.

'Retribution exacted on behalf of your weaker sisters?' His smile was hard. 'No, my suspicions don't extend to that, but what's it really all about, Blythe? Were you chosen to set me up or smooth me down? Blind me to considerations that ought to be looked at when the time for decisions comes, sway me with soft words and whatever else you use that red mouth for? Is that why Lau picked you?'

'He doesn't operate like that. Don't you even trust your own employees?' Blythe asked contemptuously. 'Of course the residents are worried about the future, and if you relocate Triple A's head office there'll be some distress, but it won't come as a monumental shock to any of them.'

'You're not a resident yourself?'

'No. My father's firm sent him out here for three years when I was a child, and, as I had happy memories of the place, I decided I'd like to work here for a few years while I still could,' she explained. 'My parents are permanently back in England now. My original job folded when the company decided to pull out of the Colony in view of 1997 and operate from Bermuda, so I joined Triple A about a year ago. If it won't add to your suspicions, I should tell you that I'm not actually either a secretary or any kind of assistant any more, although I have the necessary skills. Mr Lau borrowed me from the PR department. A lot of my work is actually done out at the airport.'

He looked her over as he had done several times before, and once again Blythe felt resentment rising.

'I should have guessed. You'd be wasted behind the scenes. What do you do?'

'Generally, liaise. With the public, the airport staff, the media when we're pushing something. I think I took a wrong turning somewhere, since I read Industrial Psychology, but I couldn't get a job which really utilised it at home or here. Mr Ballantine——'

'Christian.'

'Christian,' she tried it out, a gentle name for an un-gentle man. 'I hope all this hasn't added to the doubts you obviously have about me. If Mr Lau didn't know I was efficient, he wouldn't have risked choosing me to look after you.'

'Is that how he phrased it?' He shrugged. 'Perhaps it's accurate, since I'll require you to be more than merely an assistant, but I'm sure that was included among the warnings and gossip. Oh, I don't doubt that you'll do it all very efficiently, Blythe: be my minder, organise my life... And in view of the instructions I gave Lau, I suppose I have no option but to go along with his choice for now. Sophisticated I said, and sophisticated I've got. You're no innocent, are you?'

He was inspecting her again, and her resentment increased. She knew what he was seeing, and it would mislead him as it had Mr Lau and countless others. In this case it was intended to.

'If that's what you want to believe, go right ahead,' she invited him drily, all the warning she intended to give him. 'The people who matter to me know who and what I am. You don't.'

'I don't matter or I don't know?'

'Both.' The inexplicable anger was taking firmer hold of her now, no longer entirely under control. 'People's imaginations are so limited, bounded by the restrictions imposed by the commercial media which also shape their expectations.'

It was sad and silly, perhaps, but she had always believed it was intolerant to resent it. The standards for beauty were constantly being redefined anyway. She just happened to have the figure and features which were currently fashionable. She knew it for herself without vanity, and, if she hadn't done so, she had heard herself described often enough to be convinced of it.

'Lady, looking at you, my imagination refuses to be confined. You are, quite simply, dead sexy—a bright, silly little phrase which covers a multitude of meanings.'

'I don't exploit it,' she assured him.

'But you enjoy it.'

'Why not?'

Blythe made the most of her image with clothes and accessories, aware that in five or ten years' time her kind of looks might well be regarded as dated, and if some people thought the image was the whole and sole reality, she forgave them, refusing to stoop to the hypocrisy of playing it down. She knew who and what she was.

There was nothing new in the way Christian Ballantine was looking at her. Men did it all the time, and, mindful of what it was that had prompted Mr Lau to give her this assignment, Blythe turned a hip and posed for him, winning for herself a quick smile of genuine amusement.

'Don't be so vain,' he reprimanded her.

'If you've got it, flaunt it,' she retorted, inwardly startled by the way she was flinging herself into the act.

But she had never really flaunted it, except when she was clowning. To do so would be to make a caricature of herself.

'You've got it,' he conceded drily. 'Oh, it's all there, in the curve and sway of your hips, the indentation of your waist, the thrust of your breasts…and that smooth creamy skin which nature obviously designed to remain unblushing—or could you once blush? And you dress it all so well too, which leads me to suspect that you've been just as generously endowed in the brains department.'

Blythe had dressed with care and simplicity that day, her cotton two-piece a light, clear red scattered with a profusion of the white polka-dots that were currently her passion, the short skirt narrow enough to emphasise her hips, the short-sleeved top V-necked but covering her cleavage, while fine gold hoops glinted in her ears, her short nails were painted a light, shining red and her make-up was minimal.

'Sophisticated, Mr Lau said, quoting your orders. Did he get it wrong?'

Christian Ballantine's suspicion seemed to indicate that he thought Mr Lau had deliberately gone for seductiveness instead, for reasons of his own. Once his doubts were allayed, Blythe supposed it would cease to matter. As long as she didn't come across as the innocent poor Vicky Short had been, he would feel quite safe with her and abandon the arrogant sexual challenge with which nearly everything he said to her was saturated, presumably because he was testing her, expecting her to weaken and turn out to be just like Vicky. Did he really think he was so irresistible?

'Not so much wrong as over the top, but I suppose the man was trying to please.'

'Oh, I suspect he was thinking as much of his girls' safety as your peace of mind,' Blythe volunteered sweetly. 'The Vicky Short business was apparently traumatic for everyone at Triple A, and he's a fatherly man, who takes an interest in his staff's welfare and happiness. He's very protective of the younger members.'

And he had obviously looked at her and decided that out of all those capable of acting as Christian Ballantine's assistant, she was the best able to look after herself.

And she was, Blythe reassured herself emphatically, even if he had got certain other things wrong.

'Oh, you've got it,' Christian said softly again, uninterested in Mr Lau's qualities as a boss. 'How old are you?'

'Twenty-three.'

'And still too young to resent such a question. But old enough in every other way, and millennia of knowledge in those eyes you keep hidden so much of the time. How did you find time to acquire it in just twenty-three years? Ah, but I suspect you were born with it, weren't you?'

'Are you testing me, or is this way of talking habitual, something you automatically switch on whenever you're in female company?' Blythe demanded. 'If it's the former, I can promise you I'm immune; if it's the latter I suppose you can't help it.' She abandoned her pose and gave Christian her best, brightest PR smile, adopting her most efficient tone. 'Here are your house keys. If you'd like me to come in with you, you can tell me what's required. I went through the house this morning, and I've installed a small supply of basic foods and drinks. Everything is working, and the place has been kept regularly cleaned and aired by a domestic services agency, but you'd better let me know what you want to do about household staff, if anything. I understand that you got rid of the last lot.'

'You make it sound as if I did so in a fit of pique,' Christian commented as they mounted the tiled stairs that led up to the front door, pretty panels of delicately stained glass flanking it.

'Didn't you?'

He shrugged. 'They got in the way. Tell the agency to keep sending someone, preferably at times when I'm out. I don't know how much I'll be here, but when I am I want the place to myself. The same goes for whoever's been looking after the garden.'

'It's lovely, isn't it?' Blythe commented.

On steeply sloping land, interspersed with sheer, rocky drops, nearly everything necessarily cascaded, great sweeping tumbles of greenery and delicate falls of colour, and Blythe wouldn't have minded getting to grips with it herself. Since coming to Hong Kong any gardening she did was on a small scale, and she missed her parents' garden on which she had continued to lavish her imagination and talent at weekends even after she had left home.

'I suppose it is,' Christian agreed, pausing to glance back at it and sounding slightly surprised.

Unprofessional as it was, Blythe couldn't resist slanting him a pitying smile.

'You're really on a different wavelength from us lesser mortals, aren't you? But I suppose having several homes tends to diminish the importance of ownership.'

He glanced at her as he unlocked the door. 'Two, to be precise. I got rid of the place I had in the States as I'm going over less frequently now than when things were still getting off the ground, and for shorter periods of time. But to tell you the truth, neither the place I've got in England nor this one—which I've hardly used—feel like home to me, and the house in which I grew up was sold when my parents retired to Jersey.'

'Poor little rich boy,' Blythe murmured with mock sympathy.

For a moment irritation showed, but then a sudden blazing smile transformed him, making her draw a startled breath, because the light eyes, surrounded by long, intensely black lashes, had grown brilliant with ironical acknowledgement.

'Ah, Blythe, I'm beginning to understand why Lau picked you. Most women melt on the spot and vow to dedicate their lives to making a home for me.'

'You don't have much respect for women, do you?' Blythe followed it with a casually dismissive shrug, her own long lashes screening the anger she felt. 'I'm not sure if I have either, if they're silly enough to take you seriously.'

Christian's smile died abruptly as they entered the house, the coolly tiled entrance hall airy and light, containing a minimum of furniture. Going through it that morning, Blythe had observed that the house was comfortably and tastefully furnished, those items of furniture which would be most in use positively luxurious, but she had found it all very impersonal. It needed someone living there, long-term, scattering evidences of his personality, before it could be a home, beautiful as it was.

'A mistake you'll never make,' he commented.

There was a subtle underlying warning there—unless he was issuing a challenge.

'Not when you dramatise yourself. You see, I grew up with parents who did that,' she informed him sharply. 'In competition with each other, moreover. When I was little, I used to be frightened, thinking our happy home was breaking up, but I soon realised it was only the plates and stopped taking it seriously. But my mother has never had a complete dinner service.'

'Then our childhoods don't have much in common,' Christian commented drily. 'My parents were always very buttoned up. Even when they disagreed, it was politely.'

'Your father started Ballantine Holdings, didn't he? I read somewhere that it was a small but secure enterprise confined to the UK until you took over from him and made it multi-national.'

'Yes, he backed certainties——'

'Whereas you take risks, picking up dead-beat concerns such as Triple A was when you acquired it, just for the challenge of it, and turning them round into success stories,' Blythe recited.

'You know my lines.' He was sardonic.

'Oh, yes.' She faced him with her hands on her hips, her smile openly taunting. 'Because they are lines, aren't they? Lines for the ladies. Why don't you stop testing me, Christian, and accept that Mr Lau picked the right person for the job?'

'I've never before met anyone who managed to combine so much sexiness with so much smugness! Has it ever occurred to you that you're riding for a fall, young lady?' Something had annoyed him, and his smile was back to that cynical twist of the lips it had been earlier. 'So I'm not a challenge to you, little madam, although I warn you, I've scores more lines I could try, but has it occurred to you that I might find you a challenge?'

Consciously, it hadn't. Blythe had really thought he was testing her, and she hesitated, with the disconcerting sensation of advantage slipping from her grasp.

Christian laughed, the triumphant note incensing her.

'Why are you surprised, Blythe? Are you so easy that you're unaccustomed to men regarding you as a challenge?'

'So why waste your lines on me?' she returned acidly, recovering and declining to gratify him by contradicting the gross assumption. 'What sort of security do you want me to arrange for you?'

His mood altered abruptly to disgust. 'None.'

'You're well known, a millionaire, I'm told...' She lifted a shoulder. 'One possible danger could be kidnapping, but I imagine that after only a few hours any prospective kidnappers would be offering to pay us to take you back. What about women scorned, though? Have you thought of them?'

'Hong Kong isn't exactly littered with them.'

'There's at least one.'

'That little girl?' Christian was contemptuous. 'I think I could handle her, don't you? But obviously you have a lurid imagination. What were you envisaging? A knife in the dark? Perhaps if you've never had a man turn you down you can't be expected to know, and I don't suppose you have, but the fury bit is a myth.'

He was so callously indifferent that for a moment she felt the fury herself, on behalf of all those women he had rejected or discarded, but second, saner thoughts brought the realisation that, pity them as she might, she couldn't help also despising them for being stupid enough to let this selfish, self-centred man hurt them. .

'No extra security, then. Perhaps you'd like to go through the house with me and tell me if there's anything I've omitted to do or supply.' She changed the subject somewhat abruptly.

'I'm sure there isn't, but if there is I'll give you a list tomorrow,' he said impatiently. 'I don't feel like doing it now.'

About to add self-indulgence and obstructiveness to the derogatory mental list she was compiling, Blythe hesitated, noting the faint shadows smudged beneath his eyes and a certain nervy tension. Compunction pricked at her. He had flown in late that morning from Taipei where he had spent twenty-four hours engaged in exploratory talks with a commercial radio station in need of rescue and revival, and he had come directly from Kai-Tak airport to the Triple A, or 'All Asia Air', city headquarters, where he and Mr Lau had closeted themselves for a couple of hours before a late working lunch with the entire upper echelon of the hierarchy.

'Do you want a drink?' she asked quietly. 'Mr Lau said you weren't teetotal, but I got plenty of soft drinks in as well if you're dehydrated.'

'Alcoholic,' he decided emphatically. 'Where did I used to... Through here. What would you like?'

Having assumed that he was the sort of man who would expect women to wait on him, especially those in his pay, Blythe was surprised when he poured for both of them and brought the mineral water she had requested over to where she stood at the window in the elegant lounge.

'Don't forget you're having dinner with Mr Lau and his wife at their home tonight,' she reminded him as he raised his glass. 'Shall I organise a wake-up call for you in case you fall asleep? And are you sure you don't want the chauffeur at all? I'll leave you my phone number in case you change your mind, or think of anything else.'

'Why, where are you off to?'

'Home, when I've finished this. You won't be wanting me tonight.' She saw his quick, suddenly wicked smile and returned it tauntingly. 'Well, you won't.'

'You're right, I couldn't do you justice. But why don't you join us at the Laus'?'

'Because I wasn't invited.' She paused. 'I know Mr Lau said you might require me to act as a hostess for you, or partner you at anything official if you arrived solo, although I'm assuming you'll be remedying that, but tonight is informal, a personal courtesy.'

'And if I invite you?' he probed idly. 'Purely for the pleasure of your company, of course.'

'As I think you probably mean feminine company generally rather than mine specifically, use your little black book.' Blythe let him see her guileless eyes. 'You have got one, haven't you?'

'I suppose you counted the notches on the bedpost when you were here earlier?'

'I looked for them. I made the bed up for you, incidentally.'

'Now I'll never sleep tonight!' grinned Christian.

'Is this another test? The outrageous flirt.'

'No good either? I'll have to think of something else.'

'Don't bother.'

'Change your mind, come to the Laus' with me so I can continue working on it,' he urged her.

'To what end? Anyway, you're too late.' Blythe sipped her drink deliberately. 'I already have a date.'

'You would have,' he conceded drily. 'A regular?'

'What? Oh, no, he's a pilot, so he's not in Hong Kong all that often.'

'One of ours?'

'No.'

The blue eyes gleamed derisively. 'I'd hate to malign airline personnel generally, especially when I have so many working so hard for me, but some of them have quite a reputation. They play hard too, but I don't suppose you need telling.'

'A girl in every airport? No, I don't need telling. I can take care of myself.'

She took care of herself by only going out with men like Ward Smith, she reflected ironically.

'I'm sure you can, Blythe,' Christian allowed very softly, and something there unnerved her a little. 'Ah, well, I suppose I'll have to resort to the little black book.'

Suddenly concerned, Blythe looked up at him, as she must to see his face, her height being the only average thing about her, as a long-ago boyfriend had once told her with fulsome flattery. He probably deserved to make a fool of himself in view of the way he treated women, she reflected, and if he didn't know what had taken place during his absence from Hong Kong then he was likely to do so.

But if he had cared about Trish Biddulph, the local socialite for whom he had rejected Vicky Short, then hurt would be added to his humiliation.

'Christian, do you know?' she asked in a soft impulsive rush. 'Trish Biddulph got married soon after you left Hong Kong last time. It was in all the papers because she's so well known.'

'Yes, I know, she wrote and told me. Some sort of journalist, isn't he, foreign correspondent for an American paper?'

Abruptly, Christian's smile faded and a look of such disgust entered the light blue eyes, hardening and silvering them, that Blythe found herself taking a retreating step and placing her glass on a table for safety's sake.

'What have I said?' she asked in surprise. 'It's not the news about Trish Biddulph—or Crewe, as she is now. Obviously you knew and don't care.'

Or he had trained himself merely to *appear* uncaring, but she doubted that. It just confirmed what she had suspected. A playboy, he used women. He might reject the vulnerable, virginal girls like Vicky Short, but he probably had just as little real interest in the more sophisticated women he did involve himself with. When he moved on, they were probably as hurt as the others, only they hid it better, with too much pride to make an exhibition of it after the manner of Vicky.

Trish Biddulph Crewe had probably even married on the rebound from her affair with Christian. After all, her American husband was twenty years older than her and reputed to have a drinking problem. Blythe had seen photos of Rollo Crewe, his fifty-year-old's face ravaged either by alcohol or too many foreign wars.

'Why did you think you should tell me?'

Christian's voice was caressing, silkily so, but his eyes were narrowed as they rested on her small creamy face, and Blythe felt inexplicably threatened.

She achieved a nonchalant shrug, saying indifferently, 'I just wasn't sure if you knew, that's all.'

It failed to appease him. If anything, his regard became even more inimical, almost as if he resented her.

'Don't ever patronise me, Blythe,' he warned her softly, and she felt an inner tightening, as if her senses clenched in wary resistance to whatever danger he presented.

She let her lids drop to hide the confusion his incomprehensible anger had caused.

'I made a mistake, obviously, but I don't think it was in patronising you. It was in thinking that you might, just possibly, have feelings,' she murmured, the delicacy of her tone a taunt. 'I'm sorry, but I'll be sure not to repeat the offence. Now, I must be going.'

Christian was silent for several seconds as she glanced at her flat gold watch, before saying more naturally, 'Let me drive you, or ring for a taxi?'

'You're tired. No, I think I'll walk and then take the tram down,' she decided, a final glance through the window tempting her as the afternoon was turning into a beautiful, still evening. 'I'll see you tomorrow.'

He accompanied her into the hallway and opened the door for her, his hand brushing hers as he took the card bearing her home and office numbers which she had extracted from her small white shoulder-bag.

Blythe had frozen, and so did he as he looked at her again after sliding the card into his breast pocket. Her teeth were clenched behind her full lips, making her look both sultry and sullen. The same thing had happened when they had shaken hands as Mr Lau introduced them earlier that day, that same sparking sensation, beginning where he touched and travelling, an inward journey, to some still, secret centre of her being. It was that which had incensed her even before Christian had said a word.

Christian was immobile, but she sensed that it was an alert stillness that held him, and that his clever mind was racing, drawing conclusions. Then he was lifting his hand, laying it lightly on her bare forearm, and her skin seemed to take on a new, acute awareness, sensitised, warm and slightly damp, as if her very pores opened themselves to absorb him, expanding to receive whatever message his touch transmitted.

His hand was dark against her creamy-brown flesh. Blythe's eyelids felt heavier than usual, so that it was an effort to raise them and meet the pale brilliance of his eyes in which the pupils contracted to pinpoints and then dilated, while her own eyes grew sensuously slumbrous.

He took his hand away, his laugh of satisfaction shockingly harsh, abrasive to her sudden vulnerability.

'So that's it! I've got it. There was no need for lines.'

'But that's too easy, Christian,' she rallied, knowing it would be pointless and a lie to offer a denial, and her sardonic acknowledgement was almost a whisper, drifting smokily from her lips. 'So where's the challenge? For either of us? Have a nice evening.'

CHAPTER TWO

'BLYTHE!' Maggie Huang, editor of Triple A's monthly in-flight magazine, looked up as Blythe paused beside her desk. 'How's it going?'

'Badly,' Blythe responded succinctly.

'Christian Ballantine?' Maggie's long black eyes sparkled. 'As difficult as ever?'

'Worse. Yes, I know how I sound, but my loyalty is to Triple A's Hong Kong staff, not the Great White Chief who's suddenly deigned to honour us with his presence for the first time in over a year.'

Additionally, having resolutely contained herself in the face of the severe provocation presented by his unpredictable temperament over several days, Blythe needed an outlet, and Maggie, always sympathetic, was one of her closest friends here.

'You seem to be keeping him in some sort of order, anyway,' she was saying encouragingly now. 'So what's the problem?'

'His mood.' Blythe grimaced slightly. 'The man arrived in a difficult mood, and he's stayed in a difficult mood.'

'Perhaps it's an allergy of some sort?' Maggie had recently got into naturopathy.

'To me,' Blythe agreed darkly, but she thought it was really the opposite of an allergy and yet strictly impersonal, an automatic reaction to her sex.

Maggie laughed, not prepared to take that seriously. 'He's not in today, is he?'

'No, that's why I'm on my way out. I've been summoned to the house on the Peak.' Blythe's mood lightened and she laughed. 'Perhaps I scared him into staying away yesterday when I mentioned that Vicky Short was still with Triple A. I don't think he'd realised, as the office he's using isn't anywhere near her department, so they haven't encountered each other as yet.'

'Let's hope it stays that way,' Maggie returned fervently. 'You weren't with us yet when it happened, were you? What a performance that was—sobbing her heart out, accusing him and Trish Biddulph of just about every iniquity under the sun, threatening to kill herself... and poor Mr Lau buzzing around like a demented robot, not knowing who or what to deal with first, and Mrs Keng trying to shoo us all back to our offices, as if we weren't human. Christian Ballantine was absolutely furious, and I don't blame him.'

'He'd probably given Vicky cause,' Blythe retorted. 'He has a way of talking, and he's aware of women, almost indiscriminately, I think, and doesn't bother to hide it. He may even have been actively encouraging her until he realised how innocent she was and decided Trish Biddulph was more his kind of woman. Vicky's a lovely girl, after all, with that model's figure and her hair and eyes. I've only encountered her once or twice, and I suppose my impressions were coloured by all the gossip about the old scandal, so she struck me as being a bit of a baby, and that whispery little-girl voice as being appropriate to her silliness over Christian, but no one can deny her beauty, and Christian would definitely have reacted to it, at least to begin with. He was probably keeping his options open by flirting with her, until he discovered she'd fallen in love with him. Apparently he's incapable of tender emotions, so I suppose his preference for sophisticates like Trish Biddulph is understandable.'

'Yes, at least they possess sufficient poise to hide it if they do get hurt,' Maggie agreed.

A little later, as she drove her Nissan Sentra through the cross-harbour road tunnel, heading for Victoria, Blythe's soft mouth tightened irritably as she caught herself speculating once more about Christian's legion, legendary affairs. It was annoying to find herself so intensely aware of the man, and so curious about every aspect of his life and personality.

Even more infuriating was the look of diabolically sardonic knowledge that taunted her every time she looked up to find him watching her. Christian knew she wasn't indifferent to him, but he had made no attempt to act on that knowledge, so she supposed he had reflected on her assertion that she was no challenge to him and had decided that she was right.

Which was just as well, and made it easier for her to handle her inconvenient fascination and the odd, nameless tension that existed between them.

It was there as usual, immediately they set eyes on each other again. In jeans and a casual open-necked shirt of some soft, unbleached natural fabric, Christian was studying a long roll of paper on the patio, which was built like a platform, protruding out over the steep hillside.

'This is getting ridiculous,' Blythe snapped as for several seconds he simply looked at her, intent gaze absorbing her hair, her face and the way she wore her clothes.

'Yes, it is,' he agreed significantly.

'I meant the way you always look at me.'

'Why? Don't you like being admired?' His voice had dropped to an outrageously seductive level.

Blythe stirred resentfully, aware that the way he looked at her was just another manifestation of his intense masculinity. He might not respect women, but he was pleased by them, by the differences between their femininity and his maleness.

She was wearing a cool fitted top with a skirt that was a profusion of soft, swirling pleats in the same fabric, the clear peacock shade relieved by a snowstorm of tiniest white dots. The whole was a contradiction, both concealing and revealing, making a mystery of her body while permitting some tantalising clues, yet it was still utterly suitable for the office where she had expected to be working that day.

'It's not exactly flattering when I know it's just a reflex action. I don't know why men like you get a reputation as connoisseurs. You're not a connoisseur, you're a junkie!'

Christian's face had tightened. 'Do you really know that, or are you making easy assumptions? It may surprise you to know that there are women in the world whom I happen to like as friends, nothing more.'

'It does surprise me,' she snapped, a little startled by his palpable resentment. 'What woman could regard you as a friend when you've got such an obvious bedroom complex? You've got bedroom eyes, a bedroom voice, and everything you say has bedroom connotations.'

'I suspect the handicap is yours, lady.' He was angry now. 'But then I don't suppose you have much experience of mere friendship between the sexes, do you? There are those who claim it's impossible, but they're the ones obsessed with sex.'

'Are you asking me to be your friend?' she enquired, mockingly sceptical, and his abrupt, angry laugh was acknowledgement enough.

'No, I am not.' Christian's mood altered abruptly and he demanded irritably, 'What took you so long?'

'I paused to gossip,' Blythe confessed baldly, sighing inwardly as she accepted that his mood of the last several days hadn't undergone any improvement.

'About me, I suppose,' he inferred flatly.

'What an ego! Who else?' she conceded, smiling widely.

'Were you strictly gossiping or merely listening to gossip?' he wondered contemptuously.

'Oh, this time I was doing the gossiping. You should really dismiss me for disloyalty, not to mention the disrespect I'm showing right now by talking to you like this.'

'But then you don't respect me, do you?' Christian accepted musingly as she hooked her shoulder-bag over the back of a cushioned, wrought-iron chair close to the round table. 'So what sort of rumours have you been spreading?'

'Hardly rumours. I merely mentioned what a vile mood you've been in ever since you arrived—or is it a permanent condition? Oh, and I suggested that I'd scared you off coming to the office by telling you that Vicky Short is still with Triple A. I'd temporarily forgotten the other girls who've been sent out to us when you wanted to get rid of them, or I'd have dragged them in too.'

'I've probably already walked past the lot of them, Vicky included, and failed to recognise any of them,' he retorted callously as Blythe sat down. 'All the same, I've decided that it might suit me to work from here occasionally. It's not a bad place as houses go, and perhaps it might start to feel more familiar, a home, if I spend more time here. I've asked Lau to organise someone who can set up a computer here, or is that one of your many talents?'

'No, although I helped when we changed from green to amber on our display screens,' Blythe told him.

'Lau says it's an experiment?'

'He worries about his girls' eyes, so he keeps up with all the research, and amber is currently in favour as doing least harm, although I don't especially like it. Am I going to have to come up here every day, then?' she added, her imagination running distrustfully over several possible reasons for his decision.

'Not every day. Is it a problem?' His casual tone was suspect.

'Not really. I live on the island, so it will cut down on travelling.' Blythe was equally casual, determined not to gratify him by protesting.

'Where?'

'Down at a more modest level than this, although I've also got a view of the sea from my back windows.' She glanced down at the vividly blue sea, its further reaches dotted with tiny outlying islands like brilliant green jewels, while the harbour waters were abustle with craft of all shapes and sizes.

Christian looked at her thoughtfully but didn't comment on her evasiveness, and Blythe wasn't sure what had prompted it, since it was pointless. He could find out where she lived quite easily if he wanted to.

He said, 'Nevertheless, I'll have to get out quite a bit if I'm going to gauge the economic mood and expectations of the Colony.'

'I don't see how you can hope to do that,' Blythe said candidly. 'Hong Kong has a confidence-based economy, so the dollar goes into a tail-spin at the whisper of a rumour, and the nearer we get to 1997 and the surrender of Britain's lease, the more frenetic everyone gets. The Stock Exchange goes through some really volatile phases.'

'I need to get some idea, though.' Christian stirred impatiently. 'And goodness knows how long it's going to take me.'

The faint shadows that had marked his face on the
day of his arrival still hadn't entirely disappeared, Blythe
noticed, wondering sardonically how and with whom he
had been spending his evenings.

'Why do you need to rush at it?' she asked. 'I thought
you planned to spend some months here.'

'That was the original intention,' he admitted ironically. 'I woke up one morning a while back and realised
that I'd been working solidly without any sort of break
or holiday for what felt like years when I could quite
safely have delegated a lot. So that's what I decided to
do, before I got to the point of thinking myself indis-
pensable. I thought that here in Hong Kong, with only
one concern to absorb me instead of several, I'd manage
to relax a bit in between attempting to come to a decision about the airline's future. Maybe I should simply
get rid of it and leave the decision as to whether to relocate the central operation to whoever takes over while
I get out of here.'

'Why do you want to?'

'You know why, Blythe.' The light blue eyes were
excessively brilliant and diamond-hard as they rested on
her face. 'If there are thousands of miles between us, it
will free me of the need to come to a decision about
you.'

Shock jolted through her and she dropped her eyes
swiftly.

'No, I didn't know,' she stated caustically. 'What have
I done? I have to assume that my work isn't up to
standard, since the decision to get rid of me or not is
the only one you have the right to make without my
participation or consent.'

'You know damn well it has nothing to do with your
work. Why pretend you don't? For all your talk, you
must be well aware that the effect you have on men is

no mere reflex action. What have you done? You're still doing it, and you'll go on doing it for as long as I keep having to see you,' Christian went on derisively, following it with a disgusted laugh. 'And it appals me. You're not my usual style at all. As you've said yourself, where's the challenge? I have only to touch you and you'll be in my bed—and the fact that that's precisely where I want you makes me despise myself. It's so easy—too easy.'

'Meaning *I'm* easy?'

In the end, she wasn't really all that surprised. Most men who only looked at the outward packaging wanted her in bed and made the assumption that they could have her there.

'Aren't you?' Christian prompted contemptuously. 'I have only to look at you. If you think you're hiding it by hiding your eyes, you're wrong. You've seen it all with those secret eyes, haven't you? You've done it all, had it all... For interest's sake, just how many men have you had, Blythe?'

'For all you know, I may live like a nun.' She was scathing, playing for time until she understood how to deal with this.

'Yes, a measure of caution if not complete celibacy is forced on us these days, isn't it? Have you found it very difficult?'

'Have you?' she countered, and let him see her smouldering eyes. 'I can feel your contempt from here, Christian. Aren't you being rather hypocritical in view of all your affairs, and those strictly with sophisticated, *experienced* women?'

'I haven't had so many.' He stirred frustratedly. 'Don't you understand the essential nature of reputations? Yes, I've been involved with a lot of women one way or another, but comparatively few have been lovers.'

'You don't even give them that to go away with?' Blythe challenged blisteringly. 'But now that I know you a little better, I can believe it. You don't have much to give at all, do you?'

'Oh, I've got nothing to give the Vicky Shorts who seem to concern you so much for some strange reason,' he allowed, and gave her a blazingly arrogant smile. 'But I've a lot to give a woman who *is* my lover. I expect a lot too.'

'A challenge, for a start.'

'Yes.'

'Which I can't offer,' she pointed out.

'No, but then you don't fit into any of the categories known to me,' he conceded, and paused a moment. 'Perhaps that's why it's hitting me so badly.'

'Could be,' she agreed indifferently, but a red rage filled her mind, only her inability to comprehend it preventing her unleashing it.

She shouldn't be this angry. She had dealt with flirts, womanisers and the plain conceited in the past without allowing them to infuriate her like this, so why should Christian Ballantine evoke such a strong response, so at odds with her inherent tolerance?

'Very badly. It's new.' Christian's eyes rested on her deceptively composed face and Blythe thought she could detect a burgeoning resentment in their depths. 'On the whole, I think the best solution would be for me to succumb gracefully, forget those aspects that are bothering me and for us to sate ourselves with an affair.'

'A minute ago you were talking about running away,' she reminded him, striving to keep her sudden agitation out of her voice.

'I can't!' The faintest note of despair finally convinced her that this was no test. 'What do you think, Blythe? Shall we go to bed and discover each other's

mysteries and rid ourselves of this tension? I want you.
I want to know what you do with that ripe red mouth
and those smooth little hands.'

'And end up despising yourself once you've found
out? I can spare you that, Christian,' Blythe told him
sweetly. 'You see, it wouldn't suit me at all to have an
affair with you.'

'Why not? Are you already having one? Where does
the pilot who's not a regular fit in, then?'

'He doesn't. No, I'm not already having an affair, but
I don't want to have one with you either.'

'We needn't let it disrupt our working relationship.'

'The way Vicky did?' she taunted. 'It's not that either.
You don't suit me.'

The dark face tightened. 'Don't I, Blythe? When I
touched you that day we met—merely touched you—
you wondered what I was like in bed, didn't you? And
you've been wondering ever since, and wondering why
I've been resisting touching you again. I've seen you
watching me from under those drowsy eyelids of yours.'

'Oh, yes,' she granted him ambiguously. 'Quite
possibly. But carry on resisting the temptation, Christian,
and you'll have your self-respect intact as your reward.
You'll have to. I'm not getting involved with a man like
you.'

'If you're referring to my reputation, aren't you the
one who's being hypocritical now?' Christian was
definitely angry now.

'Oh, it's not so much all your affairs or so-called
affairs, although they do come into it. It's everything
else you are,' she asserted. 'Most of all, you're difficult—temperamental. I think I've mentioned my
parents to you, the shouting matches, the flying
crockery... I used to watch them and promise myself
that I'd never get involved with anyone like that. You're

like them, Christian, up and down. I've had evidence of it these last few days. You even threw a pen two days ago.'

'Frustration,' he quipped harshly. 'If we——'

'No, you'll still be the same person even if I do relieve your frustration,' she interrupted tartly. 'You know that. You know yourself. I want a man whose moods stay on one level, someone——'

Blythe broke off, realising she was about to launch into a description of that fantasy man she had yet to meet, the calm, loving man who was going to be her husband and the father of her children some day when she found him.

'Someone placid? I don't believe you!' Christian paused and sudden, delighted realisation chased the angry scorn from his face. 'Oh, Blythe, I know what it is! You could have thought of something more convincing, though, but I suppose it will serve. It's very generous and clever of you, to try to provide me with the challenge that's missing, but then you must be very skilled at catering to men's whims, whether with games of pursuit or other specialities. What else can you do, and how long can you spin them out, the tricks to intrigue and tantalise? So you resist and I pursue? Is that the script?'

Astonished, amused and finally angered by the arrogance that had led him to place such an interpretation on her refusal to have an affair with him, Blythe drew a resolute breath.

'I don't even like you very much, Christian,' she stated.

'What has liking got to do with it?' he questioned her dismissively. 'All right, Blythe, we'll play the game you've devised and enjoy it. The only thing that bothers me, recalling your reaction to the slightest of touches the day we met, is whether you can sustain it long enough to add a worthwhile measure of spice to the chase. How long can you keep it up?'

It bothered Blythe too, for the same reason, because she had had to accept that she wasn't physically indifferent to him, and far more urgently since, however Christian might choose to delude himself, believing the lady meant yes when she said no, this was no game. She had no intention of ever, ever adding herself to the list of his conquests and becoming just one of a number, fading to blend into part of whatever composite woman existed in his memory when he moved on.

She had told him nothing but the truth. He didn't suit her at all, and it was infuriating that she should be so powerfully attracted to him.

'Forever,' she answered him tightly.

Christian's gaze narrowed as he heard her.

'Keep it a game, Blythe. Don't make it a fight,' he advised her. 'Or is that what you like? Perhaps it's not me you're trying to please, but yourself.'

'Oh, I'm pleasing myself, Christian, but not in the way you think,' she told him sharply. 'Don't you have any work for me to do?'

'There's no hurry now that I've decided to accept my fate.' His lips curved cynically. 'We have months ahead of us for work and play. Will you come out to lunch with me somewhere? What about one of the floating restaurants at Aberdeen? We can drive round and take a sampan out.'

'No, thank you,' Blythe declined the invitation smartly.

His smile grew more intent.

'I think you're afraid,' he accused her lightly, pushing back his chair and standing up. 'I think you also doubt your ability to keep this thing in play, especially if it really is just for my pleasure that you've embarked on it.'

Blythe lost her temper, thumping a small fist on the table. 'Christian, I've told you——'

'You invented it. Let's see how long you can keep it up.'

Christian had been moving indolently away from her, but now, unexpectedly, he spun round, pulling her up out of her chair and away from the table.

It took Blythe several seconds to recover from the shock of it, and following the shock came a heightened physical awareness of him, making her realise the vulnerability of her position. He wasn't that close to her, but his hands grasped her bare arms, just above the elbows. That was all, and yet she was instantly alert to him, warmth creeping through her.

'This is against the rules,' she warned him huskily, and he laughed, a hard, reckless sound.

'Oh, no, Blythe, there are no rules in this sort of game, or if there are then I want to make some of them. It's a game for two, after all.'

'I'm not playing.' She summoned a brightly defiant smile, unaware that it challenged.

'I don't think I want to either, now that I'm touching you.'

He moved her closer, so that she felt his light breath on her brow, stirring the cluster of loose shining curls that tumbled over it. He was exerting no force, no real pressure even, and she wondered why she couldn't seem to summon the will to move away, but to do so struck her as alien, a wrong move in conflict with the dreamy fatalism that suddenly held her in thrall.

'So let's drop it,' she suggested acidly, needing him to end it for her because she could not.

'Why you, I wonder?' Christian spoke broodingly, ignoring her. 'Why you, specifically? What have you got? What makes you so spectacularly sexy, so desirable that

I must want you in conflict with everything I know and believe about myself? You're just a shape, after all, an arrangement of features... Is there anything else?'

'Not a thing,' she answered him promptly, appalled by the grudging note that had entered his voice as he went on, musing given way to resentment, but too anxious to extricate herself from what had become a perilous situation to dwell on it. 'I'd bore you in five minutes.'

'Somehow I don't think so.' He paused. 'Because it's more than just your body, scarlet lips and that trick of keeping your eyes hidden. There's intelligence, wit...and I think there might even be kindness. The whole is always greater than its parts, anyway. But does it ever bother you, the way men must look at you and want you instantaneously, without even knowing the rest, the things I've had an opportunity to discover over the last few days?'

'And assume they can have me. I'm used to it.' Blythe's voice was sharp, but free of bitterness. 'I'm not a victim, Christian.'

'I did wonder about that,' he admitted, and she was a little surprised that he should have sufficient imagination to have done so. 'So you're saying you've exercised the right of choice? You determine and control what you are.'

'I am what I choose to be,' she confirmed.

'And where you choose to be? Now, this moment, in my arms?' he prompted, his arms sliding round her to make it true.

Ever since he had laid hands on her, Blythe had been striving to subdue the languorous tide of warm sensation that worked its slow, seeping way inward from her flesh, but now her head drooped suddenly like a flower bending in final submission to the elements. In another moment, she would break.

'Don't do that!' One arm was removed from across her back, the other slipping to her waist and drawing her closer while hard fingers forced her chin upward. 'I want to kiss you.'

'Perhaps you'll find you don't like the way I kiss,' she quipped, but her voice had a fine, strained sound as her inner tension became intolerable.

'I wish to God that I would,' Christian grated with a sudden, brief upsurge of hostility.

Eyes half closed, she could look no further than his mouth, accepting the reality of the sensual curve of lips she had spent days deliberately thinking of as merely cynical. The pressure to let go, to let herself taste, became unbearable and, sighing, she surrendered, lifting her face, eyes closing completely now.

Her lips had parted and Christian's mouth covered them, warm and immediately erotic. The fingers at her chin had slackened, and now they slipped lingeringly down her throat and trailed across her delicate collarbone, tightening again on her shoulder as her soft lips trembled beneath his. The tip of his tongue nudged slickly at hers, winning a sinuous, flickering response, and he deepened the kiss instantly, probing now.

Her mouth had tingled and then taken fire from his, a slow fire which began to creep insidiously through the rest of her, heating her blood, threatening to consume. Her hands drifted to Christian's shoulders, fingers straying compulsively to the warm sides of his neck and then moving round to caress its back. She scarcely knew what she was doing. This had never happened to her before. Her mouth had never felt so hot, her mind had never seemed so detached from her corporeal being, floating away from her, out of her reach.

Other men had kissed her and she had responded with enjoyment, but there had never been this searing temptation to indulge herself fully, to relax the caution she had always known she must exercise or become the victim she had just denied that she was.

'But I do like it,' muttered Christian, freeing her mouth. 'And you?'

Too much, Blythe realised, snatching frantically at straying intellect for a moment even as her hands, fingers entwined now in black hair, smooth and sensuous as strong silk, were urging him back to her. Her resentfully protesting murmur changed to one of pure appreciation as he complied, resuming his slow, sensual exploration of her mouth.

At the same time his hands began to move about her body, making a leisurely, wandering journey, flattening themselves against her spine, and travelling on, seeking the pert, firm curve of her bottom and then the evocative, femininely receptive line of her hips. Up and down they roamed, scaling slopes with lingering delight, pausing knowledgeably at hollows, devastating as they went.

Somehow, between them, they had been confining what was happening to a languid absorption of each other, acquainting themselves with the physical realities that had tantalised, observed but unknown, for days past. Now, simultaneously, they wanted more. The questing hands burning Blythe through the fine, soft fabric of her garments had become a torment, and the discoveries her own involuntarily roving hands were making exacerbated it. The pleasurable tautness of her breasts became an ache, a need for more and greater closeness, with all barriers discarded, flesh on flesh.

Her hips stirred, signalling the quickening at the heart of her womanhood, jerking upwards to press against

Christian in eager, unconscious invitation. At the same time a faint tremor ran through him, his body taking virile life in affirmative answer to the blatant summons of hers.

His mouth slid heatedly over her small, decisive chin and followed the taut line of her arching neck as she flung back her head, finally coming to the hollow at the base of her throat, tongue probing erotically for a moment before he spoke, the low vibration of his voice setting up a matching vibrancy in her.

'Let's forget about games and go inside. Now or next week, it's going to happen, so why not now?'

Small whimpering sounds were coming from Blythe, although it took her several seconds to realise that she was responsible for them, and at the same time Christian's prompting penetrated the remoteness of her desire-drugged mind.

'Oh, no,' she refused him on a soft gasp. 'Oh, no, Christian, it's not going to happen.'

She was disengaging herself swiftly, an adept of many years, although the act had never come so costly before.

Christian let her, but he kept his hands on her shoulders so that their physical awareness of each other remained unbroken, a pulsating welter of attraction, so real, so tangible, that it even seemed to have special colours of its own in Blythe's mind, a shimmering, iridescent link.

She raised her eyes to scorch him, but the damage was to herself. Christian looked so utterly and potently male, aggressively so, face dark and eyes glittering with the urge to dominate, that she experienced a moment of atavistic apprehension.

Then it passed. Christian Ballantine might have scant respect for her sex, but he was millennia evolved from his ancestors. His women must come willingly to his cave.

'Is teasing part of the game?' he wondered roughly, lifting his hands from her shoulders to cup her creamy face for his scrutiny, but she had already half hidden her eyes from him again. 'Fool that I was to think that what's between you and me needed the fillip of a challenge, and doubly fool to tell you so. It's superfluous. It will be challenge enough simply to pleasure you, my lady.'

It was an oddly old-fashioned phrase, but somehow so evocative of erotic delights that Blythe stirred restlessly, her lips parting, redder and more tender than ever. She lifted her hands to grasp his wrists, meaning to pull his hands away from her face, but instead found her fingers straying caressingly over his bare forearms and taking a healthy delight in the slight soft abrasiveness of the fine dark hairs scattered over them.

'Just stop it!' Furious with herself as much as him as she realised what she was doing and registered the havoc and awe still rampant within her, Blythe was for once incapable of achieving anything approaching sophistication. 'Get your hands off me!'

'But it's you who's handling me,' Christian pointed out wickedly. 'So who's winning?'

He was enjoying himself, she realised, incensed.

'No one,' she snapped.

She was relieved when he finally obliged her, releasing her and turning away briefly as a slight rising breeze teased at the roll of paper on the table. It gave her an opportunity to finger her lips curiously—as if they might not be the same pair they had been before he had kissed her, she taunted herself savagely. They were, only fuller than before, and throbbing slightly. It astonished her that they should be so sensitive. Other men's kisses had frequently left her lips numb, and she could have done with that effect now, instead of this——

Appalled, she discovered that she was imagining herself still kissing Christian, kissing his mouth, his face, the dark arms her hands had so recently caressed, the flesh his clothing hid from her; kissing him all over. She could visualise herself doing it, *feel* herself...

Her hands clenched into fists at her sides and she almost welcomed it when he faced her again and she had to stop thinking about increasingly wicked kisses in order to concentrate on what he was saying.

'I think we could call the first round a draw, don't you?' he submitted conversationally. 'You've succeeded in prolonging the challenge, while I now know with absolute certainty that this thing is mutual.'

'The first round? I don't think much of the pugilistic metaphor,' Blythe retorted tartly, disturbed by the truth of the last part of his claim. 'As if we were prizefighters. What's the title at stake? Champion fool of the world? And there's brain damage to be considered.'

'Oh, I don't think there's any danger of that, although there might be other damage. Our brains hardly come into it—or mine doesn't, since I'm ignoring the objections it's raising,' he added with a revival of his earlier disgusted resentment. 'But obviously we're both going to be winners at the end, Blythe.'

She shook her head, giving him a wide, taunting smile.

'It just hasn't occurred to you that I might be serious, has it? That I might actually mean it when I say I do not want to have an affair with you?'

Christian laughed softly. 'You're dedicating yourself to all this quite wholeheartedly, aren't you? Don't carry it too far, will you? No, if I'd had any doubts before, the little interlude that's just occurred would have stilled them completely. Your response to me was a promise of delights to come, even if you are deferring delivery. Just don't spin the game out too long, or I'll cheat.'

'There was no promise, Christian,' Blythe insisted sharply, but he only laughed, knowing better.

CHAPTER THREE

BLYTHE crouched beside her miniature fountain, smooth tiles still warm beneath her bare feet at the end of the early August day. She hadn't bothered with sandals when she had come down from the house on the Peak and changed into sizzling pink shorts and a brief white top, spotted with bubbles in a multitude of rainbow colours, which tied beneath her breasts and left her midriff bare.

Behind her, the door and every window of the simplex flat were open, allowing the lilting strains of Offenbach's Barcarolle on her compact disc player to reach her softly, while in one corner of the prettily bosky little courtyard two folding wooden chairs stood open next to a matching table bearing a single glass of white wine and an English-language evening newspaper.

Everything required to enable her to enjoy the twilight time in her favourite way, whether solitary or in company, was in place, her flowering shrubs in bloom and filling the evening with their scent. Even her fountain was miraculously working, but Blythe was angrily disturbed, with a sense of being in danger.

Christian Ballantine was intent on making her his lover. So had other men been before him, and she had grown skilled in turning them away in a manner which inflicted as little damage as possible to masculine pride, occasionally to the extent of revealing more of her inner self than she cared to.

She had had plenty of practice—but none whatsoever in the art of resisting a man who attracted her, simply because none had ever affected her as Christian did.

But he was what he was, so she had to. She couldn't risk any sort of personal involvement with him, even if only on a physical level. It would be irresponsible, jeopardising the future she planned for herself. Somehow——

At this point in her thoughts the attractively painted cascade of pottery bells high above her jangled softly. Her courtyard, or garden as she preferred to think of it, was virtually a well, since another unit existed above hers and on the level of the communal driveway as the complex was built into a hillside, so a flight of tiled stairs led down to her unit.

Looking up, she felt her heart give a great agitated leap within her and her limbs suddenly went weak, so that it was an effort to rise from her crouching position.

'What are you doing here?' she called up to Christian Ballantine, who was casually dressed but carrying a jacket.

'Pursuing you, of course,' he returned blandly.

'I wish you wouldn't.' She paused, shrugging resignedly. 'Come down, the gate isn't locked, just latched.'

It was a small wrought-iron gate which she had installed at the top of her stairs for security, and Christian latched it again before descending to her level.

'Why do you?' he picked up on her first caustic statement on reaching her. 'Did you imagine the game was to be confined to office hours, Blythe? That it went with the job? It doesn't.'

'And you won't have me dismissed if I refuse to play?' She gave him a rare direct look, accompanying it with her sassy smile.

'You've really got a low opinion of me, haven't you? If you'd refused, I'd accept it. But you're not refusing, are you?' he added confidently.

'You won't believe that I am,' she qualified sharply.

'Because you're not. Why did you make a mystery of where you lived?' he asked. 'It was a simple matter to get your address.'

'I know. I realised that at the time.' Blythe frowned. 'I don't know why I did it.'

'To intrigue, of course,' Christian supplied amusedly. 'Part of the plot. It's a very simple scenario you've chosen, isn't it? Playing hard to get. Have you used it before, or am I the first?'

'Obviously, if I'm as easy as you think.'

'Why the sharp mood? You should be mellow, relaxed, in these romantic surroundings—and looking so lovely too. Who are you dressed for?'

'Not for you, anyway. If you'd let me know you were calling, I suppose you'd have expected me to slip into something seductive? For round two.'

'That's quite seductive enough.' Christian's eyes went to her top, which left the upper swell of her firm breasts and the delicate hollow between on display. 'I'm not sure how long I can endure this, but when I do make love to you it will be all the sweeter for the waiting. This is an attractive setting you've chosen for yourself,' he added. 'The complex is fairly new, isn't it?'

'Yes.' She was glad of the digression to a neutral subject, although his abrupt departure from the personal surprised her a little and she wondered at its cause. 'The privacy suits me. No one here sees their next-door neighbours, only their upstairs or downstairs ones, depending on which level we're on. I'm lucky. Mine are an extremely quiet Cantonese-speaking couple with what I think must be a model baby, as he's almost as quiet as they are. I hardly hear them, although I was warned that I should never live below anyone as sound filters downwards.'

'Is that why you chose a downstairs unit? Or don't you bring your conquests home?' Christian paused to let the subtle implication sink in, and Blythe hid her eyes swiftly. 'And the little garden? Your own work?'

'Yes. I had to get permission, of course, but my landlord seems to like what I've done, and my neighbours often stand and admire it. The upstairs units only have the walkway from the car-port level and then the balcony. I'd never laid tiles before, but I got a book on the subject, and so far the grouting has held.' As she gradually became caught up in sharing her enthusiasm her voice took on lighter, natural notes. 'The fountain doesn't always work, although that's something I'd tried before at my parents' place at home with one of those millstone arrangements. I like a water feature. I've got little low-watt spotlights hidden among the shrubbery so I can enjoy it all after dark, but Ward helped me with those.'

'Ward?' he queried.

'The pilot I occasionally go out with.'

'So you do bring them home,' Christian commented. 'And set them to work. Clever Blythe, to settle for so practical a return for your favours, especially as I'm sure you manage it so that they're left believing they're doing you a favour instead of fulfilling their part in a commercial transaction.'

Blythe's glance slid to the glass of wine on the table as sheer rage gripped her and she knew an almost over-powering temptation to fling it at his head as she had so often seen her mother throw things at her father during the height of all the sound and fury that attended the meaningless, adrenalin-charged quarrels from which they both seemed to emerge emotionally refreshed.

It would be so satisfying—but so like her parents.

Suppressing the urge, she said tautly, 'Ward doesn't owe me anything.'

'That's right,' Christian commended her amusedly. 'Never confirm or deny. That way you keep us guessing.'

'And leave you with your illusions?' she prompted softly. 'Only you think you know the reality, don't you? That I'm a pro? Christian, I'd have to be.'

Drenching it in significance, she gave him a tartly direct look and saw the arrogant dark face tighten fleetingly as he absorbed her meaning, but in the next moment he had relaxed, laughing sardonically.

'Not with me, lady,' he disagreed. 'If you must tell lies, keep them subtle enough to deceive.'

Her pout became more pronounced as she hid the rage mixed with unease that his confidence occasioned.

'Do you really think you're going about this in quite the right way?' she enquired, idly indifferent, after a pause. 'And you're only going about it . . . pursuing me, as you put it, just as if you were on safari with me as your prey, because you're piqued. You're not used to being refused, are you?'

'You chose the game, Blythe,' he reminded her abruptly. 'But I'm writing some of the rules. Insult me and I'll insult you right back.'

'And still expect me to invite you to sit down and offer you a drink, I suppose?' Blythe shrugged fatalistically, ruefully aware that at some level she was getting a strange, dangerous buzz out of their conflict. 'I only keep white wine, beer and soft drinks.'

Smiling as if he had secured victory, Christian said wine would suit him, but instead of taking the seat she indicated he followed her into the simplex, halting abruptly just inside the entrance, looking around him curiously. The walls were washed with a deep, warmly glowing cream while several dark green indoor plants in attractive containers were all lush and healthy, and an Oriental rug was flung casually over the tiled floor. A shining wooden kist, at a comfortable height for sitting on, was the only item of furniture.

'Who's the child?' he asked in a strangely reluctant voice, his expression suddenly complex.

Blythe's eyes followed his to the squint-eyed old teddy-bear sitting propped up beside the telephone on the kist, his waistcoat a faded floral silk, his bow tie as askew as his patchy old face. She laughed.

'I am. I've got lots of teddy-bears, and paintings of them too.' She indicated the watercolour on one wall, each of the three panels showing a different angle of the same dumpy, lovable girl bear, the pastel colours so soft they gave the illusion of being faded with age. 'There are more in the lounge. I suppose you could say I collect them, but I have to fall in love first to want them, and the most lovable are the oldest and so way beyond my means. They don't acquire character until they've been through a lot of loving and neglect.'

Aware of an incomprehensible tension continuing to hold him for several seconds, she had paused at the lounge door so that he could look in and see the handful of bears in there, a few wearing an elderly garment of some sort, one missing an eye, while more small pale watercolours of similar toys adorned the walls.

'I suppose they all have names?' Christian's tone was beyond her powers of interpretation as he followed her into the kitchen where another worn little bear in a broderie anglaise apron presided from the top of the fridge.

Blythe slanted him a mysterious glance. 'Secret names.'

'Like T.S. Eliot's Practical Cats?'

He sounded faintly taken aback and she was amused, aware that many people found her interest in teddy-bears inexplicable or even odd. A sophisticate like Christian was likely to be one of them.

'Not quite. My bears aren't inscrutable enough to be sitting around contemplating such things as singular names. Their history is written all over their faces—but their names have stayed the secret of their original owners, and I wouldn't presume to replace them. I think most of them would just have been called Teddy anyway. That was my own bear's name.'

Christian was surveying her with appreciatively gleaming eyes as she opened the fridge, and he laughed softly as she turned to offer a bottle of white wine for his inspection.

'Congratulations, Blythe. You've surprised me, and it's far more effectively tantalising and challenging than all the manufactured resistance. Teddy-bears!'

'I suppose you visualised me collecting something more along the lines of those plaster casts the rock groupies are said to have gone in for in the Sixties?' Blythe challenged caustically.

'An art form to which I'd never lend myself,' he quipped. 'But how can I know what sort of erotica you might have hidden in your bedroom until you invite me to see for myself?'

'Oh, go and have a look by all means, but you'll excuse me if I don't accompany you,' she returned pointedly.

'I'd probably find your own original teddy-bear occupying pride of place,' he decided shrewdly, and she gave him a small, tight smile of acknowledgement. 'Do you turn his face to the wall when you're entertaining? No, there won't be anything overtly erotic. When you can have the reality, who needs replicas...images?'

'*I'm* an image.'

It emerged spontaneously, out of an incomprehensible need to warn him. There *were* men whom she warned, of course, those in whom she sensed acute vulnerability, or the peculiarly sensitive sort of male pride that took real damage from rejection, but an arrogant playboy like Christian Ballantine didn't merit such consideration, and she felt annoyed with herself for the impulse.

'An infinitely desirable one—and I'm beginning to be intrigued by the woman behind the image.' Somehow the words contained their own warning, and Blythe experienced a wary inner clenching, resisting intrusion. 'Who's the Perrier for? You had a full glass of wine outside, didn't you?'

She gave him a taunting smile. 'Christian, with you around I need to keep a clear head.'

'And your wits about you?' he teased complacently.

'You did warn me earlier today that you might cheat. Shall we go outside again?'

'What plans did you have for the evening?' Christian asked when they were seated outside in the soft humidity of the evening air, Blythe's fountain chuckling softly beside them.

'None that involved you,' she answered him, sliding him a cautious look from beneath her eyelashes as she sipped her Perrier.

'And the pilot? What did you say his name was?'

'Ward—Ward Smith. No, he's not in town.'

'Who else is there?'

She shook her head. 'No one.'

There was a satisfied quality to his silence that enraged her, making her wish she had lied. Then he said, 'Then come out to dinner with me.'

'No, thank you.' Blythe's tone was emphatic.

'I've already semi-accepted the invitation on your behalf.'

He didn't bother to inject a coaxing note, and Blythe raised her eyes, remembering that she worked for him. 'In what capacity?' she queried.

He laughed. 'In your capacity as the woman I'm pursuing.'

'Then my answer stands.'

'Why? You'd be quite safe, you know. Since we won't be alone, I won't have the chance to claim my prize even if your performance slips and you allow me to win round two,' he taunted. 'You see, my old friend Trish Biddulph—Crewe now—rang and invited me to meet her and her husband for dinner. I told her about you, and she was curious enough to want to meet you and suggested that I bring you along.'

'I suppose you gave her the impression that you had the right to just do that?' queried Blythe.

'I merely hoped,' he corrected her lightly, but she suspected his sincerity. 'Change your mind, Blythe.'

'Why should I?' But, for a variety of complicated reasons, she was weakening.

'I need you with me,' he claimed theatrically, aware of it.

'For moral support?' she prompted sceptically.

'A man has his pride.'

She laughed disbelievingly. 'This is the cheating you warned me about, isn't it? The day we met I made the mistake of being concerned, thinking Trish Biddulph's marriage might have hurt you in some way. You didn't like it at the time, I remember, but now you're prepared to play on it. But I know you better now, Christian.'

'Except that you don't really know me at all, lady— which may be just as well. You really were concerned that day, weren't you?' he murmured, studying her curiously before shrugging. 'All right, then I simply want to show you off.'

Resentment flared. 'A wish to which you might—just might—have the right if I'd made some sort of commitment to you and could also make a reciprocal claim on you.'

'If the commitment is only temporary, it's not really commitment, and we're hardly talking permanency here, are we?' he prompted harshly, lips twisting.

Like all dedicated playboys, he needed to make sure of that, Blythe guessed sardonically. They ran at the mention of wedding-rings and mourned each time a friend was lost before the altar or in a register office. Christian's preference for experienced, sophisticated women was typical of the breed, a safety precaution.

'You're quite safe,' she assured him mockingly.

'In the sense you mean, I suppose I am. We both are.' He gave her a complicated smile. 'So you'll change your mind and come and meet the Crewes with me, won't you?'

His confidence incensed her. 'What does it take to make you accept that for once in your spoilt life——'

'You're afraid,' he accused her, a calculating gleam in the light eyes. 'You're afraid that, if you spend too much time with me, you won't be able to sustain your act, keep the game in play.'

Her eyes flashed in response to the challenge.

'All right! I've always wanted to see Trish in the flesh, anyway. She wears wild bows in her hair and tartans that belong to no known clan.' She saw the triumphant glint in his eyes too late, and added, 'Oh, very clever, Christian! Just don't try it again.'

'Because you'll be ready for me?'

'Precisely.' Blythe refused to give him the satisfaction of a panicky withdrawal of her impulsive commitment. 'I suppose Trish married Rollo Crewe on the rebound from you?'

'No!' The quick temper with which she was already familiar darkened his face. 'I've never hurt Trish, and if you even hint to that effect in front of her husband, I swear I'll make you regret it, Blythe.'

'You're overreacting.' She wondered a little at his defensiveness. 'I wouldn't do that. I must shower and change if we're going out,' she added.

'Take your time.' He was relaxed once more, his smile taunting. 'You've got plenty, as I allowed longer than this for persuading you. I didn't think you'd capitulate so easily.'

'It's curiosity, not capitulation,' she reminded him, and he laughed as she stood up. 'Help yourself to another drink if you want it, read the paper, play some music, whatever you like. I won't be long.'

Something was out of control, Blythe reflected as she showered in her bathroom, its warm honey-coloured tiles going right up to the ceiling, a small steam-proof picture of a teddy-bear left out on a beach above the bath.

She supposed she was giving ballast to Christian's belief that they were engaged in a game and that she fully intended to let herself be caught in the end. It was a form of teasing, something she despised. When she went out with a man she was careful to let him know where both he and she stood, because she was aware that her looks did tease. She had no mission to punish the men who mistook her, setting them up and knocking them down, and she had always felt slightly ashamed of those of her sex who did that.

But Christian had provoked her!

It was his own fault, if he later believed she had been leading him on—and it was a conclusion that was inevitable, since she had no intention of spoiling her future by getting involved with a man like him. He had only himself to blame. He shouldn't have challenged her like that.

She shrugged mentally as she dried herself, watching herself in the big mirror with the indifference of familiarity. She had nothing to feel guilty about, although she was disgusted by the way she had let him goad her into agreeing to spend the evening with him. She would be on her guard from now on, so there was no danger to her—and none to Christian either. He wasn't one of those men she felt compelled to apprise of the truth. He could discern it for himself or not, and probably the latter, since Mr Lau's choice of her as his assistant would appear to confirm that she was what she seemed.

No, nothing was seriously out of control after all, she decided with a complacency she thought was confidence as she left the bathroom which adjoined the simplex's only bedroom. She could cope.

She put on silky white underwear and wriggled into one of her typically paradoxical outfits, the light airy fabric extravagantly feminine, patterned with minute white dots on palest eau-de-Nil, the skirt frivolously floaty, the short-sleeved jacket tailored but made dramatic by the way the neckline plunged between soft revers to display a hint of cleavage, and romantic by a touch of white lace.

She was fastening it when Christian knocked at the bedroom door, which she had left ajar because he had put on an Andreas Vollenweider CD which was one of her special favourites soon after she had left him.

'There's a bathroom off the entrance hall,' she told him abruptly, her heart giving a little jump.

'I wanted to see,' he returned, coming in.

'You're too late.' She did up the last button and turned herself slowly round in front of him.

'Your bedroom. You did say earlier that I was welcome to have a look.'

He was laughing at her, and Blythe was suddenly sure he was aware of the tight breathlessness that afflicted her.

'No mirrors on the ceiling, I'm afraid,' she told him.

In fact, her bedroom was warmly feminine without being frilly, floral curtains and the thin quilt on her bed matching cane-edged papered wall panels, apricot shades with subtle touches of delicate green, the painted sections of wall adorned with the occasional small watercolour or drawing, not only of teddy-bears but also such other old-fashioned toys as rocking-horses, dolls and dolls' houses in bamboo-type frames to complement the casual furniture.

'Nice big bed, though. And there he is, as I knew he'd be. Teddy.' Christian strolled towards the chair on which lolled a squashy-faced bear, somewhat older than Blythe because an eager grandmother-to-be had anticipated not merely her birth but her conception. 'Better loved than any of the men in your life, I suppose.'

'Of course.'

Blythe held her breath as he picked the bear up, but there was respect in the way the elegant hands held it.

'And you must have loved him very well,' he realised whimsically, studying the worn patches on the battered face and an arm that swung too loose and which he carefully put back into position on replacing the toy on its chair. 'But it will have to be my place, Blythe. I think I might find those beady eyes inhibiting when I make love to you.'

There was something indulgent in the look he sent her, and Blythe stiffened in defence of her individuality, wishing furiously that he had never come here, invading her private space, finding her out.

'We won't be making love—and I hope you don't think you're uncovering a case of arrested development here,' she added sharply. 'Simply, I like—what I like, that's all, even if I haven't put away childish things.'

'Other than the traditional bear, the things of your own childhood would have belonged to the plastic era. Those with which you've surrounded yourself belong to an earlier generation, and to me they reveal both a reverence for history and for craftsmanship, as well as a very adult discernment—particularly the Ernest H. Shepard-type sketches of kids with kites and hoops that you've got in your little dining area, my intrusion into which I hope you'll forgive, even if the only excuse I can offer is curiosity.'

That was all right, then, Blythe found herself thinking before she could catch herself up and dismiss her irrational relief. It didn't matter what Christian thought of her, whether her peculiar interests turned him off or not. She just wished something would turn him off!

Lowering her gaze, she slipped her feet into high-heeled sandals and moved towards her dressing-table.

'They are like the Shepard illustrations, aren't they? I used to love A.A. Milne, especially the books of verse. I've still got them back in the UK. They were my grandmother's originally.'

'Has someone laughed at your hobby, Blythe?' Christian enquired almost gently.

'No...'

And she hadn't really been afraid that *he* might either, she reassured herself positively.

'Then why let it worry you?' he went on, his voice dropping caressingly as he followed her across the room and, watching his lithe, easy progress in the mirror, Blythe was prey to a sensation of being stalked. 'You're quite blatantly adult and very, very much a woman— almost shockingly so. I imagine there are men who feel intimidated by that, and they must find your innocent, idiosyncratic, almost homely collections reassuring rather than amusing.'

Blythe jerked a shoulder dismissively. Christian himself was one man she could never intimidate, but nor would she let him intimidate her. All the same, she wanted him out of here. There was something too intimate about his presence in her bedroom.

'How much time have I got?' she asked shortly, lifting the lid of one of the pretty boxes scattered about her dressing-table, containing her jewellery and other small accessories.

'There's no hurry. Your parents?' he asked, indicating a small, obviously amateur photo, and she nodded. 'No one else? Were you an only child?'

'Yes.'

'A lonely only?'

'Not really. Is this curiosity about me part of the game?' she queried.

'Don't the rules allow me to be interested in the things that have gone into making you what you are?' Christian retorted impatiently. 'Do you really think I'm so crass as to limit my interest to your body and nothing else? That makes you crass, Blythe.'

She shrugged, disconcerted by a feeling that he was right. 'I just wondered. No, I suppose the only times I felt a bit isolated were when they were having their fights, because they were . . . very personal things, just between the two of them, so I couldn't join in; I was just an onlooker, never a participant.'

'I think I'd have liked that. I was also an only, and whatever was personal and private to my parents' relationship was just that—very private. Feelings, the emotions, however positive, weren't a subject for discussion in our family. Perhaps it was a kind of confidence, though. I don't know.'

'I suppose I'm luckier than many people in that mine are so uninhibited,' she realised aloud. 'I was always also an audience to their declarations of love once the interminable storms blew themselves out, as they always did, and they obviously found making up highly satisfactory. Sometimes I thought they started their quarrels solely for the fun of ending them. But they were tedious, all the same.'

'And I suppose you were terribly superior about them,' Christian prompted. 'I see you as one of those unspeakable adolescents, smugly confident that you were going to organise your life much better than your parents had done theirs.'

Blythe gave a small dry smile of partial acknowledgement. 'I took them too seriously, anyway.'

And now she was taking Christian too seriously—or she had let the conversation get too serious, anyway. They were talking about real things, things that really mattered, and somehow that was far more disturbing than the sexual innuendo which had previously characterised their conversations.

'But I think I'd have preferred your parents' sort of restraint,' she went on lightly. 'Obviously something got swapped around somewhere and we got the wrong sets of parents.'

Christian smiled, watching as she held up a string of crystal beads to her throat, studying the effect in the mirror.

'No,' he said abruptly, the smile fading, 'don't fill it in. That part of you needs no adornment.'

The return to such trivia was a relief to Blythe. This she understood and could deal with.

'You're really taking a lot for granted, aren't you?' she challenged him sweetly. 'But I'll give you the benefit of the doubt and assume that my sex is to blame, as we are for so many of the chauvinistic assumptions men make. But if the women in your life have really given you the right to believe you can dictate what they wear, then you're even more spoilt than I thought.'

She would have liked to put the beads on, simply as a gesture of independence, but annoyingly, he was right. The effect would be cluttery. Reluctantly she dropped them back into their box.

'Spoilt?' Christian tested the word distastefully.

'Shockingly.' Blythe was smoothly emphatic. 'As I think I've said before, you've got it all. Nature, fate and a lot of weak-willed women have combined to make you over-privileged in just about every way there is. You've got it all, therefore you think you can *have* it all.'

'Including you, my smug little madam?' He was unperturbed by the criticism. 'Are you one of those weak-willed women?'

'Has no one ever said no to you and meant it?' she wondered, giving his reflection a brilliantly contemptuous smile.

'No one has ever said no,' he responded simply.

'I have. I am.'

'It's the word that comes out of your mouth,' he conceded. 'But without uttering another word, that same mouth gave me a very different answer earlier today. An unequivocal yes, Blythe. Yes?'

'No.'

But his hands were on her shoulders, turning her, and under his touch there was no answer at all. Her mind still functioned, issuing imperative orders, telling her to move away out of his reach, but her body wouldn't obey, simultaneously lethargic and stirring with excitement. It was as if she was physically drugged, with a lethal combination of tranquillisers and stimulants warring in her bloodstream.

She could sense Christian endeavouring to search her face, but she kept her eyes downcast, and after a moment he expelled a quick sigh which combined resignation and exasperation.

'So secretive,' he muttered.

Hard fingers moved to her small resolute chin, tilting her face upward, so she closed her eyes, feeling his breath fan her skin and knowing that in another moment she would also feel his lips on hers.

She did, but that was all. Christian's lips touched hers, rested lightly against their warmth—and remained thus. It was enough. A slow, sweet tide of honeyed sensation spread through her, the secret regions of her body quivered and her lips stirred, parting moistly beneath the waiting stillness of his.

Then she realised what he was doing and forced herself into immobility. This was a tactic in what he still believed was a game, aimed at forcing her to be the one to both invite and offer more, thus conceding him the game, or this round of it, anyway.

Blythe let him see a little of her smouldering eyes as she withdrew from him.

'If we're going out I have to do something to my face—and I don't want an audience. Out!'

'Gilding the lily.' Christian paused. 'All right, I'll leave you to your mysteries. But one of these days quite soon, Blythe, you're going to be sharing all your secrets with me.'

CHAPTER FOUR

'ALL right, Christian, I accept it. The great Vicky Short contretemps isn't about to be repeated.'

Blythe didn't think she was supposed to overhear, as Trish Crewe had lowered her voice to an intimate murmur, but her entire attention had been riveted to the pair ever since she had noticed Trish's languid white hand straying to Christian's arm and lingering there. He was wearing his jacket now, and the sight of those long red nails lying against the expensive material held a horrible fascination for her.

The restaurant at which they had met up was on the Island, at the top of one of the tallest hotels, and bar and dining area both commanded glittering views of the city. Trish and her husband had been there first, waiting at a table in the bar, and Rollo was currently making his way back from ordering drinks for Blythe and Christian.

Something savage was tearing at Blythe as she stared at that caressing hand on Christian's arm, and she wondered wildly if she was going to be taken suddenly and violently ill before realising that the thing rending her so shockingly was emotional rather than physical in origin.

It left her feeling momentarily bewildered and inexplicably trapped, but then anger surfaced.

Christian had discussed her with Trish. They had speculated about her together, and Trish had evidently issued some sort of warning which she was now retracting.

64

'Your drinks won't be long,' Rollo Crewe said, sliding into his seat beside her again.

Blythe gave him an acknowledging smile, but found her gaze swivelling to Christian and Trish almost immediately. Trish was said to be thirty and she was classically beautiful, with pale skin and Nordic grey eyes, yet the style she affected was the opposite of classical. The platinum blonde hair was cropped short and currently sporting a big silvery bow, and her dress with its crossover bodice would have been a nightmare on anyone else. Made of some sort of silk, its wild colours were patterned into a species of tartan which Blythe thought could cause wars. Heavy bracelets jangled on her wrists, and her face was dramatically made up, eyelids a silvered statement, lips a shiny crimson shout.

A small, perfect beauty spot was situated just above those lips, and Blythe wondered if it was real.

'It comes off,' Rollo Crewe's attractive American drawl came from close beside her as he leaned towards her confidentially. 'It also moves around.'

Blythe turned to him again with a delighted smile, relaxing a little.

'You read minds?' she questioned him softly.

His crumpled, bearded face broke into a grin. 'Nothing to it, when everyone has the same thought. It was the first thing I wondered about her when I met her—and I was dead drunk at the time. It was all I could focus on.'

Rollo Crewe and drunkenness were synonymous in popular legend, Blythe recalled. He was drinking straight Perrier now, but his hands had a bad tremor, which was probably why he hadn't elected to carry Christian's and her drinks back from the bar himself.

'What secrets are you two telling each other?' Trish demanded, her attention caught by their lowered voices as a waiter arrived bearing a tray, while Christian was surveying them with hard eyes.

'I was just telling Blythe that you're a fake,' Rollo told her happily. 'There you go, Blythe. Is that OK, Christian?'

'Oh, but we all are, aren't we, Blythe?' Trish retorted, shooting her a great big smile. 'Frauds, the lot of us.'

She was no longer touching Christian, and Blythe smiled back at her, accepting that her friendliness was unedged by anything else, although there was frank curiosity in her gaze, so perhaps she really had been left unscathed by the termination of her relationship with Christian.

'In one way or another,' she concurred. 'And it's not always contrived. Nature can create the same illusion as deliberate artifice.'

'The creation is easy. It's maintaining the illusion that presents difficulties.' Trish's words slowed towards the end of the flippant statement and her eyes widened slightly as if something had just struck her.

'If you ladies are talking about what I think you're talking about, then Blythe found a very simple way of solving the problem earlier this evening, Trish,' said Christian, and something wicked in his voice made Blythe tense apprehensively. 'She turned me out of the bedroom.'

Blythe shot him a sultry look, promising him a reckoning, glad that she could remain unblushing as she saw Trish lift fine eyebrows. Christian was deliberately creating the impression that their relationship was advanced and intimate. Smiling blandly, she set out to undo it.

'That's not so easy to get away with in a *real* relationship, is it, Trish?'

Trish eyed her speculatively for a moment before laughing. 'Tragic, but true. However, I think I've managed to leave Rollo with a few illusions.'

'Whereas all of mine are intact, but then you've got something of a start on us,' Christian claimed, blatant challenge in the sparkling glance he sent Blythe. 'Which reminds me, since I wasn't able to make your wedding—belatedly, to the both of you... No, on second thoughts we'll wait until we eat. You merit a champagne toast.'

'I should hope so!' retorted Trish.

'I have to stay on the wagon,' Rollo inserted gloomily.

'What about you, Blythe?' Trish wanted to know. 'That's Perrier, isn't it? It's necessity in my husband's case, but you're young and healthy... But perhaps you don't like the taste of alcohol?'

After her initial friendliness, the saccharinely condescending enquiry was unexpected, and Blythe met her eyes expressionlessly, trying to interpret the false note, prey to a strong impression that she was being probed or tested in some way.

'Oh, it's also necessity, Trish,' Christian was saying before she could speak. 'Blythe was telling me earlier that I go to her head like wine. The real stuff in addition could be disastrous.'

'That isn't quite what I was telling you.' Blythe looked at Trish. 'You've known Christian longer than I have. Does he always interpret everything to flatter his vanity?'

'He, and most men.' Surprisingly, there was apology in Trish's grey eyes now, and a small, rueful smile played around her mouth.

'Should we separate them now or later, Rollo?' Christian asked the other man innocently.

'It's that or run, man, and I don't really fancy losing face that way,' Rollo asserted in the same tone.

'I should have known when I saw Blythe stepping into her spike-heels.'

'Ditto when Trish stepped into hers.'

'Oh, listen to it, Blythe,' Trish invited gently.

'Male-bonding?' Blythe asked limpidly.

'We learn quickly and by example, girls,' Christian offered.

'Divided we fall,' Rollo proclaimed melodramatically.

For a while the conversation remained confined to such socially acceptable sparring, giving way to other impersonal topics while they had their meal. Blythe enjoyed herself, deciding that she liked both Trish and Rollo.

At intervals, though, she found herself studying her companions speculatively, wondering who if anyone had emerged hurt from the relationship between Christian and Trish, and just what Trish's marriage to Rollo was founded on. The gossips had speculated long and avidly after the wedding, since the kindest thing anyone could say about this shambling fifty-year-old giant of a man, his hair thinning on top, was that he was a physical and emotional wreck.

'Burnt-out journalist weds madcap heiress,' Rollo murmured, catching her in the act of looking from his wife to him while Christian and Trish were discussing liqueurs with their wine-waiter towards the end of the meal.

If Blythe could have blushed, she would.

'You're reading my mind again,' she accused quietly.

'It's another thing everyone wonders—with some justification,' he comforted her, grinning. 'I usually leave them to do just that. Love, little girl.'

'Oh!' She was softly ashamed. 'I should have thought, instead of letting the gossip influence me.'

'My God, and she believes it too, the uncynical child!' he whispered to the ceiling. 'More of your kind, Blythe, and my kind would be redundant.'

'Are you still a journalist?' Blythe asked with a mocking little smile for his exaggeration.

'Sure, only now I'm what they call a "fireman", rushing out to wherever after whatever has occurred, covering the aftermath. Trish likes to call it a weaning process. From January I'll be taking up a position as bureau chief for this part of Asia. The stuff I was doing before, the bad...' Rollo hesitated, groping for a polite word, but Blythe gestured her comprehension. 'It got to be a bad scene for me, addictive. Hell, quitting all the other junk, liquor and the rest, was easier. I was a war addict and I lost something of myself—morality, a capacity for anger, but I went on wanting it, a god-damned vulture. I knew it, I hated it, but the chemicals, the weeds, the poisons—you name it—dulled the shame. I was spending some leave here—reluctantly—when I met the lady, and she dragged me kicking and screaming and hung-over across to one of the refugee camps and the Shek Kip Mei resettlement area and made me look through her eyes and feel her outrage. End of story. No book or shepherd's crook, just this kinky dame with a clown's make-up and big bows in her hair and a bossy British voice, making me feel again. Not a pretty story or an original one, although unlike others I've emerged from the other end of the tunnel and, sweet heaven, why am I laying it on a kid like you?'

The sudden embarrassment mingling with his cynical self-disgust went straight to Blythe's heart.

'Because I wanted to know,' she said quietly before becoming aware that both Christian and Trish had fallen silent and glancing at them from beneath eyelids care-fully smudged with sludgy neutral colour.

Christian was observing her with narrow-eyed, slightly suspicious interest, his mouth sardonically curved, while Trish's expression was complex, resentment just one of many emotions there. Blythe recognised it of old and was sorry for it, but the distrust of her own sex was one of the burdens she had learnt to accept long ago. If Trish really loved Rollo then it wouldn't mean a thing to her that in age he came somewhere between Blythe's own parents.

Rollo laughed with sudden good humour.

'True Confessions! I think Blythe must be going to be another bossy British lady when she grows up. She's been—what's that phrase—drawing me out?'

'She's all grown up already, aren't you, Blythe?' Trish prompted drily. 'Hadn't you noticed, Rollo?'

'I had,' Christian put in silkily.

'I only have eyes for you, my darling.' Rollo was grinning.

'Diplomacy yet, unless you've suddenly gone blind,' retorted Trish.

'Christian is younger and fitter than me.'

'So am I,' Trish said darkly, and inspected Blythe's carefully composed expression. 'Sorry, Blythe, but you must be used to it?'

'You too?' Blythe responded, relieved.

'And Christian, and probably Rollo as well in his prime. He's still got something.' Trish was relaxed once more.

'Oh, you beautiful young people,' Rollo mocked cheerfully. 'You have no idea!'

As the banter continued, Blythe was quiet, made uneasy by the way Christian was regarding her, and she did no more than sip the liqueur she had been persuaded to order with her coffee. After a while, Trish threw her a sparkling look and addressed her in the voice of a gum-chewing adolescent:

'Wanna go to the girls' room and talk about the boys?'

Rollo thought it was funny, but the look Christian gave them as they rose contained a warning which Blythe thought was directed at Trish as much as her.

Trish was filling in the pencilled outline of her lips with crimson colour as Blythe finished washing her hands and joined her in front of a long mirror softly lit with flattering pink bulbs above a marble console.

'Are you trailing clues deliberately, or was it inadvertent?' Trish asked her incomprehensibly. 'If what I think is true, you're asking for trouble. I know what Christian is like. Or is it a game?'

'*He* thinks it is,' Blythe answered the only part that she truly understood.

'But you're serious?'

'I'm not playing,' Blythe said flatly.

Trish turned and gave her a long, thoughtful look before shrugging.

'Then good luck to you—and don't worry, I won't say a word to warn him. You've got the odds stacked against you as it is, without any sabotage from me. But, Blythe,' Trish's voice had dropped, 'I'd hate to be you when he finds out.'

But there was no need for Christian to find anything out, because she wasn't playing, although it seemed that Trish had discerned the truth, or an aspect of it, in the space of a couple of hours, Blythe accepted, reflecting on the odd little exchange as they returned to the men. It was a rare occurrence, but Trish was a quick and perceptive woman, more attuned to feminine truths than a man with similar qualities but wilfully accepting the evidence of his eyes might be.

Her admiration and liking for the older woman wavered and dipped irrationally as she and Christian were parting from the Crewes and she saw Christian's dark head inclined and Trish's face raised for his farewell kiss.

The same emotion that she had felt earlier clawed at her again and, looking down, she was shocked to see that her fingers were tensely curled, as if in readiness to tear the couple apart by force.

And she wanted to! The sight of them so close together was somehow an assault, viciously bruising to something tender and vulnerable within her. She felt offended—insulted—hating Trish for touching Christian and hating him for allowing it.

This time Blythe had to accept her turbulent inner revolt for what it was, a savage, unreasoning possessiveness which, when felt with regard to a man with a history as long and varied as Christian's, could destroy her.

The instinct arose out of a terrifying chaos, raw and hot, a molten centre of emotion which, brand new as it was, still felt frighteningly familiar, patterned in her long ago.

A sensation of being trapped enclosed her again, as if she stood looking at catastrophe with nowhere to run or hide, bitterly regretting the complacency that had allowed her to come out with Christian Ballantine tonight, so confident that she could cope.

Out of control, she had thought earlier, and casually dismissed it, so smugly sure that she could come to no harm, all heedless of the dire, black practical joke she had been programmed to play on herself... *Inflict* on herself. Sexual jealousy...

Appalled by what had been waiting to confront her, Blythe was silent as Christian saw her into the Rolls-Royce.

'What did you do to Rollo Crewe?' He was silkily derisive as they joined Hong Kong's heavy night traffic. 'Something other than you've done to me—but then you're like one of those mischievous and misleading spirit beings, assuming the shape a man most wants or expects to see. Only it's your personality that changes, so, whatever form it takes, it always works, doesn't it, because the outward shape remains the very seductive reality that it is. I gather he isn't usually into soul-baring.'

'No.' A taut thread of anger ran through Blythe's voice. 'Make all the innuendoes you like about me and other men, but not Rollo Crewe, Christian. You're the one who said men and women can be friends, and it's true—even in my case.'

Ward Smith was also a friend, she might have added, but it occurred to her that Ward's presence in her life in the role Christian had automatically assigned to him might provide her with some sort of tenuous protection, although she wasn't quite sure how, and it seemed a fragile hope at best.

A little to her surprise, Christian wasn't prepared to drop the subject, or even make light of it in his usual fashion.

'Are you saying you weren't flirting with the man?' he queried.

'Just that—if it has anything to do with you.'

'Oh, it has everything to do with me. I want you to flirt with me.'

'Is that all?' She faked relief.

'You know damn well it isn't all.' He sounded uncharacteristically grim.

'And I suppose you weren't flirting with Trish?'

He took his time about answering, and when he did so he merely enquired smoothly, 'Were you jealous?'

'To be jealous, I'd have to want you for myself,' Blythe snapped, a little more heatedly than she had intended, needing to convince herself more than him, now that the initial shock of finding herself so irrationally jealous was beginning to recede.

'Don't you?'

'No!'

Christian relaxed perceptibly, laughing at the emphatic denial, but he didn't take her up on it, staying silent for several seconds before changing the subject.

'It's tough being a sex symbol, isn't it?'

'You should know.'

'Why, thank you, Blythe. As it happens, I do.'

'And don't you mean a sex object?'

'Who are you referring to? Yourself or me? We're what we choose to be.' He paused. 'You had Trish worried for a moment or two.'

'Needlessly,' she told him.

'Yes, I think you're right, whether you actually mean it or not,' he allowed arrogantly. 'There isn't going to be room or time in your life for anyone but me for quite some time to come.'

'You think! Rollo is old enough to be my father,' Blythe added a little hurriedly, anxious to divert him from the subject of her attraction to him. 'And Trish's, for that matter.'

'A very young father in her case—and believe me, that's not how she regards him. With a perfectly adequate, real live father of her own, even if he is half the world away, she's hardly in need of a father-substitute, and Rollo distinctly lacks most of the proverbial sugar-daddy assets, if that's what you're wondering.'

'It isn't. You said her father... I thought Trish was a Hong Kong resident?'

'She is, but in view of 1997 and an uncertain future her parents opted to pull out when her father retired. In fact, it was their choice of the Channel Islands that brought me into contact with Trish originally, since that's where my own parents are these days.'

'And keeps you in contact?' Blythe surmised, since she didn't think Christian was the sort of man who would generally bother to keep in touch with discarded lovers once his affairs ended unless they occupied some very special category. 'She's a family friend.'

'More than that. We're fond of each other.'

She wondered how long the affair had lasted, her mind sadistically running a movie trailer for her torment. *Scenes from an Affair.* Just one affair among how many others?

The monster gnawed ferociously. Jealousy... It was completely irrational. Christian meant nothing to her, except on an inconvenient physical level, so her reactions shouldn't be emotional. Or was this really sexual jealousy? She had thought that was a male prerogative, but perhaps women were equally capable of it. Whatever it was, it was unwelcome; she didn't need it, didn't want it in her life.

Blythe turned her head and looked at Christian's arrogant profile, sharply defined against the brilliant street lighting, and wondered what to do.

The time had come to put an end to the game they were playing, to withdraw her participation. Oh yes, she could acknowledge now, she had been playing too, under protest and yet not protesting enough, carelessly confident that no one was going to get hurt.

But the whole thing was definitely way out of control now, at least for her. Jealousy, even if it was only sexual jealousy, was a damaging emotion, and ultimately destructive.

'You are asking me in, aren't you?' Christian prompted urbanely when they were at her simplex and he was unlocking her gate for her.

'Yes, I want to talk to you,' Blythe agreed quietly.

'Talk, Blythe?' he mocked.

'Talk,' she confirmed curtly.

Inside, she switched on lights and led the way into her attractive lounge which she had furnished for comfort and pleasure, a lot of space given to books and CDs, cushions and rugs generously strewn about, the contrasting fabrics all in soft warm colours.

She looked at Christian as he came to a halt in the centre of the room, and she grew tense again. So dark, his eyes so light in contrast, he was so beautifully made, and suddenly she wanted him very badly, her whole being clenching with the sweet agony of it.

'Let your heart break while it's still young enough to mend.' It was her mother's voice, inside her head, typically urging her to emotional extravagance—but why should that particular piece of advice return to her at this moment?

It was utterly irrelevant in the present circumstances. She wasn't going to break her heart and Christian wasn't going to break it for her.

She said abruptly, 'Christian, this has gone far enough. We have to stop it. I can't play your game any more.'

'It was your game,' he reminded her, moving towards her. 'But I agree. It has become superfluous—if it was ever necessary. Lord knows why I thought I wanted the challenge of a chase in the first place. There's so much to you that intrigues as it is, and the real challenge lies in making you forget every other man you might have had while you're in my arms. We've got all night and whole months ahead of us to achieve that.'

All the time in the world—until he left Hong Kong and left her, Blythe reflected sardonically.

Christian had shrugged out of his jacket as he spoke, dropping it on to a chair, but he halted a couple of feet away from her in obedience to her upraised hand, his smile indulgent although impatience flickered in his eyes.

'You've misunderstood me.' The words emerged quick and light. 'Oh, I know I'm partly to blame. I could have done more to convince you . . . or done less. I shouldn't have gone out with you tonight, for instance, and I'm sorry to have misled you. I was never playing and it was never a game. We're not going to be lovers, Christian.'

Because she was looking straight at him in her need to convince him of her sincerity, Blythe saw both the anger and the dawning comprehension that flared simultaneously in his eyes.

'You *are* still playing!'

Just for a moment her appalled despair was unexpectedly touched with amusement at the obstinate, arrogant way he adhered to his belief that she fully intended to become his lover sooner or later, but dear heaven, hadn't she given him reason?

'You——' she began.

'Well, here's news for you, Blythe,' Christian overrode her attempt to speak, his temper well up. '*I* don't want to play any more. Did you say this had gone far enough? It has gone way, way too far. Any entertainment I might have derived from your admittedly skilled and very, very tantalising act has ceased and become frustration. Hell, I've spent the last few hours wishing to heaven that I'd followed up what I started in your bedroom before we went out, but stupidly, I decided to make a contribution of my own to your damned game, tease you as you were teasing me. I wanted you frustrated—but didn't it rebound on me, because my own frustration was was multiplied a thousandfold!'

Blythe was frightened by now, no longer capable of looking at him.

'Won't you accept what I'm saying?' she asked, only just managing to keep a tremor out of her voice. 'You don't suit me. It doesn't suit me to have an affair with you.'

'You're losing your taste for it already too, anyway.' Christian's dark head lifted in the triumph of victory. 'You did it so well to begin with, keeping it light, but there's something pedestrian and forced about your protests now, and you've run out of originality. When a game gets heavy, when the players start taking it seriously, it's time to abandon it.'

'You're impossible!' Now Blythe lost her temper, her hands clenching and unclenching at her sides with the need to throw something at him. 'If I sound too serious for your taste, Christian, it's because I am—deadly serious, not trying to amuse you.'

'Drop it, Blythe,' Christian advised her tautly. 'It's pointless; there's no need for it. There never was really, when you think about it. We're two adults who want each other, and why should we postpone our mutual pleasure by playing silly games more suited to adolescents who are secretly scared of that pleasure because it's unknown?'

Blythe was in his arms now, and she drew a deep breath, striving to counter the debilitating physical weakness sweeping through her by keeping her mind strong and clear.

'Christian, for the last time——'

'I sincerely hope it is.' A quick hard smile lit his face. 'The last empty protest you'll make—but only the first time we'll make love. Let it go, Blythe, sweet. There's no good reason for it, you want me, and you haven't got anything serious on the go at present, so...Why not?'

'A thousand reasons,' she answered him, but his hands were moving on her body and a languid note had entered her voice.

How much was she to blame for her predicament, and how much was it the arrogance of this spoilt playboy who had been taught—by her sisters, damn them—to think he could have whatever he wanted?

Realising that her hands were sliding up over his chest, seeking his shoulders, she stopped them momentarily, then fatalistically let them travel on. She wondered how she was going to extricate herself, but it was a distant, almost absent-minded wondering, a flimsy scrap of thought that went floating away from her as Christian's hands stroked over her back, burning her through the thin material of her garments.

Her smoky hazel eyes were dark slits beneath her heavy lids as he looked down into her face.

'You fascinate me,' he muttered, his breath stirring the shining clusters of fair brown curls about her brow. 'I want to know everything about you, discover every secret... You keep your secrets well, and you've got a lot. You know a lot, don't you, Blythe? But you're going to show me. You're going to show me what you do with that blazing mouth, and your hands, and your body. You're going to show me every secret delight you hide under your swathes of polka-dots, and how you love a man, and why... And your eyes, lady.'

He kissed each of her eyelids in turn, his lips light and warmly caressing. He was making love to her with words, and her body was arching pliantly to his as his hands spread and shaped themselves to her firm buttocks.

'You think,' she managed, not knowing how to get out of this but acutely aware that—somehow—she had to. 'And what are you going to do for me? Oh, I never said that!'

Blythe was shocked to hear herself. How could she hope to convince Christian of her unwillingness to have an affair with him if she came out with things like that? He could only construe it as a flirtatious response to his verbal lovemaking—and wasn't that precisely what it was, the unpremeditated words leaping up and out from that ungovernable, instinctive part of her which did respond to Christian in defiance of her sensible awareness that an affair with such a man, and based solely on physical attraction, could only lead to disaster?

'But you did, sweetest. What am I going to do for you? That's something you're going to be telling me very shortly.' His low voice caressed her. 'And you're going to smile while you do. I haven't been counting your smiles, but there are so many, each one different from the last . . . I want to see how you smile when I pleasure you, and when I excite you . . . and you're going to open those eyes for me so I can see what you're feeling when you welcome me into your body. I want all that from you, my lovely temptress . . . and my tormentor.'

The sound of his voice, scandalously seductive, enveloped her like a warm, rocking ocean, lulling her, so deceptively soothing as it dragged at her with gentle insistence, sapping her will to resist until drowning seemed the most desirable end in the world, to be sought and embraced.

'I'm not—Christian . . .' The feeble protest she tried to summon was lost, yielding before the languorous sigh of surrender which emerged shaped as his name and whispered against the firm, sensual lips nudging at hers.

Merging, their two mouths became a cavern of voluptuous delight, the erotic gliding dance of sinuous tongues and mobile, clinging lips creating a place of rich, dark pleasure. Too swiftly overwhelming to be confined or contained, it spread and spread, gathering warmth and weight and strength, stirring their bodies and heating their flesh, until it became something inexorable, sweeping through them now, growing and gaining, feeding on itself, every new thrill of sensation sparking subsequent thrills.

The slick thrust of Christian's tongue was a promise of paradise, and Blythe trembled, holding on to him and making a little moan of frustration when he tore his mouth from hers a moment later.

'It's so...*much*!' In contrast to the eloquence with which he had been wooing her, Christian was now unexpectedly inarticulate, groping clumsily for phrases with which to express himself. 'I think that must be why I've...resented it, resented you, almost, I suppose. Do you also feel that? Is it unique for you too, Blythe?'

'Oh, yes.' The voice making the admission had a fine, shivery sound, as if somewhere within her something was on the verge of shattering.

It was unique, never experienced before, desire a continuing explosion of energy deep in the soft, secret heart of her femininity.

And it had to be stopped.

CHAPTER FIVE

IT WAS her confusion over the angry, possessive emotion that had shocked her earlier which finally enabled Blythe to turn limp and unresponsive in Christian's embrace.

Had she merely been attracted to him, without all that inexplicable and tumultuous emotion to complicate the situation, she thought she might have weakly succumbed to the urgings of her flesh, but the way he had succeeded in provoking so much emotion as well was an affront, far more deeply resented than an unwelcome physical attraction, and hostility rose.

She became a rag doll in his arms, hands fallen away from him, the hot rage filling her heart and mind more imperative than the dictates of the body which still yearned to wind itself about Christian, to wrap him in her passion and take him into her pulsing warmth.

It hurt to do it, and she accepted furiously that her initial self-indulgent surrender had been as unfair to herself as it had been to Christian.

Except that he hadn't yet registered her present lack of response.

'I want to take my time,' he was murmuring against her throat, clearly intent on the upper swell of her breasts where they rose from the soft material of her eau-de-Nil top. 'But I'm not sure if I can, because at the same time I want to hurry, to have it all... What do you say? Do you ache for me the way I do for you? You haven't fainted, have you, Blythe?'

It was his first inkling that something had changed, but as yet he was incapable of taking it seriously, and

Blythe swallowed, unwillingly guilt-stricken, because how could he be blamed, given her earlier response to him?

Emotion constricted her throat, damming the words she would have spoken as he raised his head to scrutinise her face briefly.

Whatever he saw there, focusing on the bright fullness of her lips or glimpsing the feverish glitter of her half-closed eyes, either distracted or reassured him, because his mouth fell abruptly on hers again. Now, though, he became aware of the absence of movement and passion in the lips and flesh he sought to possess. Briefly, frustration mastered him; his mouth crushed hers, grinding at her lips in an attempt to arouse, and the vital potency of his hard body seemed to undergo a shift in character, becoming angry aggression instead.

They were moments of wilfulness, an obstinate refusal to accept the physical evidence, the reaction of a man women desired, a man unaccustomed to being denied. Pain, as unwanted and incomprehensible as her earlier anger, lodged itself in Blythe's breast as she withstood the brief assault with which Christian sought to impose his will and force a response from her. Her nerves, her flesh, seemed to cry out, a shrieking protest against the domination of her newly imperious will.

'No!' she denied herself aloud as he finally released her with a single, savagely disgusted movement.

'What happened?' he grated, bitter rage blazing in his eyes. 'You——'

'Yes, call me a tease and all the other things,' she invited him tautly. 'I know I deserve them, even if I didn't deliberately set out to... I'm sorry. I shouldn't have let you get near enough to touch me.'

'And how am I supposed to take such a pretty apology? My God!' He was scathingly incredulous. 'What do you expect of me? That I'll say yes, of course,

I understand your change of mood—I won't say heart—don't worry about it, and let's forget the whole thing? If this is an extension of your game——'

'There was never any game,' Blythe interrupted stonily, shame suddenly very real, forcing her to keep her eyes downcast.

'What, then? *Is* that really all you are, a malicious little tease?' Christian demanded. 'It's beginning to seem like it, except that I can't believe, on the evidence of the response I had from that hot, sexy mouth, at least to begin with, that you make a hobby of denying yourself the pleasures of lovemaking. So what was it? A whim—some sort of feminine caprice?'

'Why is there always this emphasis on gender when it comes to caprices?' Even knowing herself to be in the wrong, at least partly, Blythe still felt an answering surge of defensive anger. 'Don't men have them? Aren't I just the whim of the moment to you, the same way all your other women have been? Can you see their faces when you remember them—if you remember—or do they all blend into some sort of composite?'

'What are *you* getting so cross about? Because I'm not enchanted by your mercurial change of mind? I suppose the other men you do that to think it's charming and cute, and let you walk all over them, falling for the trick again next time you feel like leading them on a little? I'm not that tolerant, Blythe. As a matter of interest, do you do it often? Turn on and turn off? If so, I advise you to be very careful about who you bring home with you. Not every man in the world is going to smile fondly at your womanly ways and meekly trundle off home all unsatisfied after you've promised so much... But perhaps you don't mind if things get a little rough occasionally. Perhaps your appetite is sufficiently jaded to require that sort of stimulus. Was that what you were trying to provoke here?'

'You have a right to be angry with me, Christian.' Blythe's soft voice was smoky, acrid with temper. 'You do not have a right to make gratuitous and offensive assumptions about me!'

But the Ballantine temper was also well up. 'Then again, perhaps you've become so blasé about it all, about what you do to men, that you turn off the moment conquest is assured. Your vanity still requires the fillip of knowing it never fails, but anything above and beyond that proof has become superfluous. Too much of anything eventually palls.'

'Then you must be incredibly bored,' she snapped. 'But isn't all that contempt just a little hypocritical, Christian?'

'It's you who is the hypocrite, lady, in all sorts of ways, I suspect,' Christian derided harshly. 'You're also stupid. You know enough about men to know the risk you're taking, behaving as you have tonight. What guarantee have you got that I'm not going to demand that you deliver? Not to mention any other men on whom you might try the same trick?'

'I can take care of myself.' Blythe managed a dismissive little shrug. 'I wouldn't have let you come in with me if I thought you didn't draw a line between seduction and force.'

'Great judge of character—or of men?' he mocked savagely. 'I suppose you have got something to go on, but is anyone's experience so vast as to make their assessments infallible? I think you're tempting fate. I also think you're playing a very dangerous game, whether deliberately or not. Have you any idea how challenging your complacency is?'

'Confidence, and I don't mean it to be.'

'Confidence in me? What if you're wrong, Blythe?'

Christian's dark face seemed sculpted out of granite as she risked an upward glance.

'I'm not.' She gestured expressively with her hands, immaculate red nails gleaming in the soft lighting. 'Oh yes, there was a moment earlier today when I looked at you and saw your ancestors, and felt all the apprehension of my female ancestors... Does that satisfy your incredible ego? But it was a moment out of time.'

'We're so civilised now?' he taunted cynically.

'Some of us. We have standards, at least.' Blythe shook her head, suddenly struck by the incongruity of the subject and wanting to end it. 'Anyway, your overt preference for sophisticated, experienced women says everything about *your* standards.'

Christian laughed contemptuously. 'That particular preference has existed solely and simply because that kind of woman is less likely to make the mistake of falling in love with me and causing all-round embarrassment and irritation—and falling in love is hardly what we're talking about here, is it?'

The question emerged with so much angry intensity that she realised incredulously that even now he must still automatically be seeking assurances that the woman with whom he sought to involve himself wasn't going to turn out to be another Vicky. The amazing part of it all was that he still hadn't accepted that there wasn't going to be an affair. His arrogance was phenomenal!

'What we're talking about here is distasteful, and pointless,' she answered him dismissively. 'Why don't you go home?'

Christian's silent regard was hostile. Then he lifted a shoulder.

'Yes, why don't I? Luckily for you, I do happen to like my women willing, and, more than that, actively responsive. Plus, despite what I said earlier today about liking having nothing to do with what's between us, I also like to be able to... *like* them, and I can't say I like you much right now.'

She supposed she couldn't really blame him, Blythe accepted as she accompanied him into the entrance hall. She didn't like herself much either, because, when all was said and done, her behaviour tonight had been nothing more or less than that of a tease, prompted by her own earlier complacency. Much of his anger was justified.

'Tomorrow?' she questioned him expressionlessly as it crossed her mind that his dislike might well prompt him to order Mr Lau to replace her.

'The office, not the house,' he advised her. 'I've got that series of meetings you organised, so have all the data I'll need available. I may also want you to make notes. Stay inside. The particular politeness of seeing me out seems peculiarly empty under the circumstances.'

'I have to lock the gate.' Blythe retrieved her bunch of keys from where they lay on the polished kist.

'It's hardly effective as a security precaution. A nonagenarian could probably climb over it,' Christian commented as they mounted the stairs outside, the sound of Hong Kong's night traffic a continual hum in their ears and the sky above them lit a harebell shade by the city's concentrated mass of lights, sad stars invisible.

'It's a deterrent, though,' she said optimistically.

'To those unwanted would-be lovers you're so smugly confident would never force themselves on you?' He went through the gate, closing it and watching as she locked it. 'Or is it only me, Blythe? You conceded earlier that what was happening between us was unique, but perhaps you allowed me to misunderstand your meaning? Unique in that with other men you follow through, deliver what you've promised—but not with me? What is it, Blythe? Have you decided to cast yourself in the role of my Nemesis or something? Because of my reputation, all those women you seem to take such delight in referring to, not forgetting the highly imaginative multiplication you've applied to their number? It would be hypocritical of you, but I remember you said there'd be a sort of justice in it if something of the sort happened.'

She laughed scornfully. 'Rough justice, or poetic justice? But Nemesis is divine. I'm not that vain, or that arrogant, Christian. Anyway, men like you go through life all untouched by any sort of Nemesis.'

'With its reputation for aptness and irony, I'd have thought it was aimed at men like me. Men like me,' he repeated distastefully, keeping his voice low, but she felt his anger, like a field of electricity into which she had strayed. 'Just one more reference to my reputation. Have the people at Triple A been busy ever since you joined them, or only since they heard that my present visit was impending? What strikes me as incongruous is the converse restraint they exercise where you're concerned. You are what you are, it's written all over you, and yet surprisingly little of it is public property. What talk there is, is speculative. People guess, they assume—even Lau—but they don't really know. How do you do it?'

The question was so resentful that for a moment Blythe was disconcerted, and she had to force herself to remember that, even if his reputation was slightly exaggerated, he had brought it on himself. There *had* been Vicky Short, and those other girls sent out to Hong Kong to get over him or to be got out of his way, and there *were* also the sophisticates with whom his name was linked from time to time. His reputation was well earned.

She said tartly, 'I don't do it. For one thing, I'm not rich and famous.'

'On the other hand, perhaps it's my position that makes them so discreet about you when I'm around,' Christian mused.

'The big boss.'

'And *your* boss, Blythe. Don't forget that.'

Silky satisfaction replaced the anger that had ridden him ever since his discovery that she wasn't responding to him. Blythe's skin prickled as she tried to read his face from beneath the screen of her eyelashes.

'Just try it, Christian,' she warned him very softly. 'Just try using your position and see where it gets you.'

'Sued?' His even white teeth showed as he smiled fleetingly. 'No. Where would the satisfaction be, always supposing you allowed me to get away with it?'

'Then what was the warning for? Because that's what it was.'

'Warning, or declaration of intent?' Now his voice held a hard, confident ring.

'Have you still not accepted it?' Blythe demanded with weary incredulity.

'No.' He paused deliberately. 'Why should I? You wanted me before the Ice Age set in. I didn't mistake that. I believe there'll be a warming trend before too long. You wanted me, and you will again, Blythe . . . and I intend to encourage and take advantage of every slightest indication of it, in office hours or out of them— and unless all this is a very elaborate extension of your earlier game, I imagine that for the time being it's going to have to be in office hours if I'm now *persona non grata* out of them and this little gate remains locked to me.'

'Then I hope you're able to make a distinction between harassment and whatever you want to call it,' she cautioned him flatly.

'There'll be no harassment.'

Blythe looked down at her hands resting on the top of the gate and knew she had run out of answers. Resisting him earlier and then countering his subsequent anger had used up some part of her, at least temporarily. There was nothing left.

Raising her head, she gave him a rare direct look, but her eyes were blank.

'Oh, go away, Christian,' she adjured tiredly. 'I'll deal with you tomorrow.'

'No, Blythe, I'll deal with you,' he contradicted her smoothly, turning away, and to her ears it sounded like a declaration of war.

She was frightened now, she acknowledged bleakly, wandering over to her fountain and staring unseeingly at it after the whisper of the Rolls-Royce's tyres on the driveway above had confirmed Christian's departure.

Most of all, she was frightened that he might be right, that, next time he touched her, a thaw would begin.

Because——

A tiny moan escaped her as she was finally forced to accept what she must subconsciously have been fighting all evening, not daring to accept it in his presence, convincing herself that the angry possessiveness that had afflicted her on seeing Trish touch him was irrational, rooted in sexual jealousy. Oh, but she had been reacting emotionally to Christian right from the start and not just tonight, she conceded; he had incensed her the moment they'd met, and it had taken off from there, the uncharacteristic anger she had felt in his company a vivid clue to the truth.

But this was not the way she had expected to love.

She had known that once it happened it would be decisive and complete beyond all doubting, but she had anticipated a sure, gentle knowing. This was unexpected in its intensity, a raging, demanding emotion that threatened to consume her at the same time as it was directed outwards, a positive, profligate welter of feeling.

Nor was Christian Ballantine the man she had expected to love. He too was unexpected—and utterly impossible.

The painful awareness of all that loving him implied was already tearing at her, but for now fear was the greatest of her emotions. How could she deny him, and deny herself? Sooner or later, wasn't she going to find herself weakly settling for the physical semblance of love he was willing to give her, simply because she did love him and that made him irresistible?

An affair, at the end of which——

No! Blythe flung her head up. She couldn't, she wouldn't accept so little. She wouldn't add herself to the number of his casual, ephemeral affairs.

She tapped a foot irritably on the tiles. It was such an unsuitable love, this thing that had jumped her so shockingly, this *mugger*, especially in view of the terrifying possessiveness which seemed to come as part and parcel of the whole unwanted deal. How could she ever happily have an affair with a man of his reputation? Suspicion would eat her, corrode the relationship even before Christian was ready to end it.

She would never be able to trust him. Love was the only security you had in a relationship, the only certain insurance against infidelity.

Oh, but the question of any sort of relationship with Christian didn't arise, she reminded herself impatiently, simply because love wasn't involved, on his side anyway, and wasn't likely to be, since she suspected that he must be incapable of loving to have reached the age of thirty all immune to its destructive power.

What she had to do was find a way of discouraging him, scaring him off if necessary, before he seduced her into squandering her love—and oh, she ached to spend it, pour it over him, trap him with it so that he could be hers forever, all the yearnings of an unrealistic dreamer, she acknowledged bitterly, knowing Christian wouldn't want all that, just her body in his bed—and thereby accepting a victim's role.

Blythe spent part of that night contemplating ways and means, shying away from certain solutions before they could lodge in her mind and mock her. They were too final and——

And who was she kidding?

'Rough night?' Maggie Huang asked her, noticing the faint brownish smudges under her eyes when they encountered each other in one of the lifts at the Triple A building in the morning.

'On my brain, anyway. I've been trying to think of a way——' Blythe broke off, then succumbed to frustration, resuming impulsively, 'How do you frighten a playboy away?'

Maggie's eyes sparkled and her smile made her pretty cheeks pop up in her moon-face. 'Can I quote you on that?'

'Not in the magazine, for pity's sake, and I haven't mentioned any names,' Blythe said hastily, accepting that it was as much as she could ask for, human curiosity and the related tendency to gossip being what they were.

'No, of course not,' Maggie soothed her mischievously. 'And you seriously want to discourage the guy? I suppose you have your reasons. It's easy, my dear. You cultivate the furniture look.'

'The what?'

Maggie giggled. 'It's what I was once accused of by a dedicated bachelor I went out with. I started making him nervous because, according to him, I'd pause and get a certain look in my eyes every time we passed a furniture store. Oh, he was right, I was eighteen and the nesting instinct was strong. He finally ducked out of my life when, without a word of encouragement from him or even a hint about marriage, I suggested that we spend an evening making a list of who we wanted to invite to our wedding. He's probably still running... And, Blythe, I won't gossip about you if you promise not to breathe a word to anyone about what an idiot I was. Stop laughing! You asked for my advice, and that's it, culled from the wealth of my experience! What sends bachelors—playboys—running for their lives? Weddings and babies! Start looking at furniture, develop an interest in expensive rings, muse aloud about the names you're going to give your children.'

'I don't really think the situation warrants such extreme measures, but I'll bear it in mind.' Blythe looked at the other girl and laughter escaped her again. 'Maggie, I'm shocked!'

'So am I when I look back,' Maggie agreed calmly.

Blythe's mouth still quirked. 'I've always seen you as the complete, single-minded career woman.'

'These days it's how I see myself.' Maggie paused and looked at her curiously. 'You're different, though, aren't you?'

'Oh, I admire it in others, but I'm not sure if I could emulate it,' Blythe confided. 'I suppose I'm mildly ambitious and I do take a pride in acquitting myself well. I've enjoyed my various jobs even though I've never found one that utilises my degree, and they've enabled me to live, fairly well at times. I suppose I enjoy the companionship more than anything, as well as the stimulation and fulfilment, but . . . OK, it's your turn to laugh. I've always seen myself marrying and having a family to complement or balance my life.'

Last night she had said goodbye to the long-held dream of two children and a placid, loving husband.

She could spare a wry smile for her complacent idealism and then dismiss it. The dream had been discarded abruptly, with a few regrets but no struggle, because what had happened to her was so irrevocable that fighting it would have been futile.

And what was to become of her now?

'But perhaps I should consider following your example,' she added as Maggie shook her head cynically. 'I'd need to find a job I can really feel passionately about first, though.'

This one wasn't it, she reflected on reaching the office that had been allotted to her while she was acting as Christian's assistant, relieved to discover that he was not yet in his.

Add that to the fact that for as long as she remained in contact with Christian she would be in danger—of succumbing, of settling for too little—and why wasn't she begging Mr Lau to replace her or even tendering her resignation altogether?

He had looked in while she was testing all her new philosophy on herself.

'Miss Steed? *Josan.*' He beamed as he gave her the local greeting. 'No problems? You find it all coming back to you?'

'Oh, yes, sir.' She beamed back. 'Quicker than I thought, in fact.'

'Am I permitted to say I told you so?' They were talking about the only doubt she had entertained about her temporary preferment. 'And otherwise, generally?'

He was a fatherly little man who showed a natural, nice protectiveness towards all his staff, particularly the young. She might not appeal to it as automatically and instantaneously as the Vicky Shorts with their wounded Bambi eyes all uncomprehending of their own pain, but his disapproval of Christian's way of life was well known, and Blythe knew she had only to pout and murmur a complaint to be replaced—and be safe.

'No problems, Mr Lau,' she assured him.

Why? Why hadn't she asked to be returned to her official job? What was she trying to do to herself?

She was sitting staring unseeingly at her keyboard, frantically endeavouring to dodge the several unpalatable truths that beset her from all sides, battering at her resolutely closed mind, when Christian walked in.

'Good morning.'

Blythe felt quite pleased with the way the greeting drifted composedly from her lips as she slanted him a brief upward look, so it was disconcerting when she received no reply.

Eyes lowered again, she waited—and waited. He just stood there, still and silent as a statue. She could see his feet, in expensive leather shoes, planted squarely on the dove-grey carpet and the bottoms of his trouser legs, part of one of the stylish, subtly fashionable lightweight suits he wore for the office.

Eventually, slowly, needing to steel herself to do it, she was forced to raise her gaze fully, wincing inwardly when she confronted his blazingly victorious smile.

'So that's how it's done,' he mused softly.

'What?' she responded tightly.

'Getting you to look at me,' he elaborated. 'I've sometimes thought that if I grew a full moustache overnight or even underwent some horrific mutation you'd hardly notice.'

Blythe shrugged nonchalantly. 'Well, I'm looking at you now. What am I supposed to be seeing?'

'You tell me.'

Her pout became a little more pronounced as she forced herself to keep her eyes fixed on his dark face.

'I can't see any changes. You haven't grown a moustache or changed into a werewolf. You're wearing a thin blood-red tie.' It was a relief to find a valid excuse to drop her gaze. 'An aggressive colour.'

'But then I feel aggressive,' he informed her lightly. 'What about you, if we're taking symbolism here? No polka-dots today. Does the jazzy white represent peace or surrender, or was the purity it denotes meant to turn me from my purpose? If so, you shouldn't have added the flowers. They shout.'

The intense interest he took in her appearance, part of his overt appreciation of all things feminine, was one of the facets of his personality which had incensed Blythe, and she understood now that it was because it emphasised his utter masculinity. As always she experienced an inner clenching as she instinctively tried to resist its impact.

Her summer two-piece was a brilliant white, absolutely plain save for the narrow bands of lace edging wide lapels, but she had attached a small cluster of the highly realistic silk flowers for which the Hong Kong textile industry was so famous to one lapel, the idiosyncratic mix of colours, marigold and crimson, her own choice and repeated in the frivolous bangles adorning one arm.

Undermining the need to resist the magnetism of his sheer masculinity was a dangerous urge to respond, but to do so would not only be to allow him an advantage but to confirm once and for all that she was a tease, something they both despised. She had to go on fighting him, and fighting herself.

'Why do I get the impression that war has been declared?' she asked shortly.

'Because you're a clever, perceptive woman,' he suggested amusedly.

'I hardly need to be. You're not exactly being subtle about it.'

'I could be, but it might give me an unfair advantage.' Christian smiled an acknowledgement of her sceptical little laugh. 'You're dead right, Blythe. From here on, all's fair and anything goes. War is the name of the game. You've had your warning—*fair* warning, but that's all the fairness you can expect, as you've hardly dealt fairly with me.'

'Just one more time, please, Christian,' she appealed, faking a demure humility and matching it with a lightning-quick oblique glance. 'What exactly are you warning me of?'

'Do you want a list?' Something sadistic added itself to his smile. 'For a start, I'm going to uncover the sultry mysteries you hide behind those secretive eyelids, one by one, but first and most important, I'm going to find out the reasons for and the nature of the tortuous game you've been playing with me, and still are for all I know, because it was never just a challenge aimed at pleasing and tantalising me, was it? Likewise, I'm going to acquaint myself with the physical mysteries...every curve and crevice, Blythe, because you've already given me the right to anticipate the privilege. You've made silent promises with your mouth and body and hands, and ultimately I'm going to collect. I think that about covers it.'

'It's quite comprehensive,' she commented judicially over the deep interior tumult his evocative words had stirred. 'But aren't you contradicting yourself in certain ways, Christian? You talk about war, and you talk about games.'

'If it's a game, it's become my game now,' he told her.

'Played to your rules.'

'Oh, no, lady, there are no rules any more. You cheated in your game and so will I. I'm playing to win, and nothing less than complete surrender will satisfy me.'

In some terrible and terrifying way it excited Blythe. Essentially, Christian was threatening her with absolute, lifelong possession, because to yield him the transient victory he sought would be to make a loser of herself forever; she would never be free of him even after he discarded her and moved on to the next affair.

If she wasn't the loser already, loving him——

She tried to push the weak thought away, aware that the next step was to start rationalising and justifying, finding reasons and excuses for succumbing to the ultimate weakness.

But at the same time, some fiery, reckless part of her that responded to Christian ached to answer his ruthless challenge and play his game with a fatalistic indifference to the outcome—just as if self-respect, the remaining shreds of an independent identity and perhaps even her life weren't the things at stake, Blythe lambasted herself scathingly.

'And just how are you going to achieve all these goals?' she asked him in a coolly lazy little voice.

'Oh, no, Blythe, do you really think I'd tell you?' he retorted sardonically. 'And give you the opportunity to assemble a defence, devise some counter-strategy? The warning was as to what, not how.'

She found herself smiling, tartly but quite spontaneously.

'I just thought I'd slip it in, as you seem to have a penchant for describing in advance.'

'You liked it, didn't you? Last night?' Christian prompted wickedly, voice dropping to a familiar caressing pitch. 'It excited you. Oh, I'll happily tell you what I'm going to do *to* you—or *for* you, as you put it last night when you wanted to know. Would you care to hear now?'

'No, thank you.'

She knew all too well what he would do. He would, in the phrase he had used, pleasure her, beyond bearing, and take his pleasure of her and then, sated, he would move on, looking for someone new to pique his interest. He probably wouldn't even remember her very well after a while, but she would remember him. Always.

He would destroy her. It was no exaggeration. The physical fact of life would remain, but she would nevertheless wither and die, an inner dying of the spirit, because if she had to accept herself as one of a number of lovers strung like beads along the line of Christian Ballantine's existence, she could never value herself again.

She would be a precious one and only in Christian's life, or she would be nothing.

Well, she wanted to be, Blythe amended mentally, with a greater measure of humility.

Christian was smiling at her.

'It'll keep. You will,' he promised her. 'Now shall we do some work?'

CHAPTER SIX

'WHAT are you waiting for, Blythe?' Christian asked softly.

For a moment Blythe thought he was impatient to be rid of her, and she drew a breath, ready to tender a flippant apology for delaying her departure, although it was less than five minutes since the last guest had left.

Then a sidelong glance showed her the enigmatic smile curving his mouth.

'For a move that's never made,' she admitted in a strange, stifling voice that she would have had difficulty in recognising as her own, had she been listening to herself.

'Has it unnerved you?'

They were in the lounge of the house on the Peak. Blythe hadn't been able to refuse to act as his hostess at the small dinner-party which had now come to an end, since it was strictly a business affair.

'I imagine that was your intention?' she countered drily.

'Then again, I could have been trying to lull you into a sense of security,' Christian suggested.

'That should be a *false* sense of security...shouldn't it?' she added, needing to know quite urgently.

'Did you imagine I might have lost interest?'

Blythe hesitated and a tiny, involuntary smile crept and flickered round her red mouth, although she was ashamed of it and tried to contain it.

'No,' she said honestly.

'You don't suffer from false modesty, do you? That's not meant as a criticism. Why should you, when you know exactly what you do to men—what you do to me, Blythe? Now tell me what it's done to you, the waiting?'

'But, Christian,' she mocked gently, 'I've only been waiting for you to make a move so that I could counter it.'

'Ah. You believe you can? You have something planned?' The possibility didn't seem to perturb him. 'Have you been very impatient, waiting to try it out?'

'Well, it has been almost two weeks since you made all your fine threats,' she pointed out. 'And you've been circling me for all of that time, especially on the days we've worked up here with no one else around.'

In fact, she had felt like the potential victim of an unpredictable predator, trapped and at his mercy but not sure how or when he was going to spring—although she didn't imagine that Christian would actually do anything as crude as literally leaping on her. He liked to use words, to seduce, to tease, to torment.

'Has it made you jumpy?' he queried.

'Why should it?' she hedged with a confidence that didn't really exist because she hadn't been able to come up with any concrete plans for dealing with the situation when Christian did finally make a move.

'Frustrated?' he continued.

'Not that either.'

'You don't usually tell outright lies,' he remarked thoughtfully. 'And we both know that's what it is. Almost two weeks, you said; have you been counting, then, my darling? And in all that time we haven't touched each other, although we've frequently been alone together, with no possibility of being disturbed. How have we managed that, I wonder?'

'Will-power?' Blythe suggested brightly, producing her most insouciant smile while her lively heart went on reacting wildly to the endearment he had used. 'Why don't we try for a record?'

'I'm not that much of a masochist,' Christian returned feelingly. 'The only marathons that appeal to me are bedroom ones. But without our laying a finger on each other, it's still been there all the time, hasn't it? Whatever it is that's between us. We can call it attraction, if you like, but it's more than that, one of those must-have things. That's where all the tension has come from. We haven't even had to look at each other. Merely being in each other's company has been enough to set us wondering how the reality is going to compare with the fantasies we've been entertaining. Lord, I haven't fantasised about a woman for years... And the tension is here between us right now. It's time for us to try the reality, isn't it, Blythe? It's what we both want.'

Christian wasn't wearing a jacket, and as he spoke he was removing the idiosyncratic midnight-blue bow tie which Blythe had thought affected on first seeing it before conceding that it actually enhanced his devastating attractiveness, the single concession to civilised frivolities merely emphasising the animal magnetism of his essential masculinity.

Lithe and indolently graceful, he prowled in her direction now, and she was reminded of nothing so much as some complacently aristocratic cat hunting, not out of necessity, but because the instinct was bred in the blood, the thrill of the stalk and the tragi-comedy of the innocently sadistic and long-drawn-out capture the sole incentive.

The image was apt, and it was breaking her heart. Christian didn't need her, didn't hunger for her, but she had provided him with the challenge and amusement of the chase. When he had her, would he play with her until the spirit to survive went out of her? And then, tiring of the fun, wander away to preen himself, today's conquest forgotten by tomorrow?

But thwart a feline long and hardily enough and he lost interest for fear of losing his dignity, Blythe reminded herself optimistically.

But she sounded helpless, hopelessly lacking in conviction as she said, 'Haven't you got the message yet? Christian, how do I convince you?'

'Oh, I'm convinced.' Christian's voice had hardened. 'I've been convinced from the minute we met, when Lau introduced us and we shook hands and I felt you calling to me from deep inside yourself, where you want me...and where I want to be. Do you know what happened to me in that minute? What's been happening ever since, when I look at you or think of you? Of course you know, because the wanting is mutual... It's time to stop the games, isn't it? Both the games, yours and mine. We've tormented each other long enough, and needlessly. Two weeks haven't changed a thing, save increasing the frustration, and to be honest I had only the faintest hope that they might. I've been thinking about what might lie behind it all, why there's been so much hostility, or resentment, mixed up with the attraction. It's simple really, though, isn't it? There are certain things we don't like about each other, or rather, things we have difficulty in accepting, and so we've turned desire into a weapon of aggression. I regret that. We haven't been kind to each other. It was myopic of us, an emotional reaction, when the single positive aspect of our relationship is so overwhelming that we can afford to ignore the negatives. They don't matter—we can't *allow* them to matter any more.'

'What can you be saying, Christian?' Blythe was close to panic, now that he had reached her, but she managed to make it mocking. 'That this thing is bigger than both of us? Hardly original.'

'But then great truths seldom are,' he asserted equably. 'They've been truths too long.'

His hands came to rest on her bare shoulders and she went very still, but only outwardly. Behind her ribs, her heart was fluttering wildly, while her brain raced, seeking solutions in between wondering just what it was that he found unacceptable about her.

'Ward Smith is in town,' she tried, unusually gauche, but it was all she could think of for the moment. 'If I hadn't had to *work* tonight, I'd have been spending the evening with him.'

'The pilot?' Christian's smile was hard and brilliant. 'He doesn't count. Whatever he's been to you in the past, he's no longer the man you want, and we both know it. Duty or not, you wanted to spend the evening with me, and all the other evenings we've denied ourselves with our nonsense. You dressed and scented yourself for me, not our guests, although I noticed that they all sustained severe damage. Look at you! You came here tonight, quite blatantly a woman who'd prepared herself to come to a new lover, dressed to be undressed.'

Blythe drew a shivery little breath as light, warm fingers trailed over her shoulder-blades. Resentfully, she supposed that at some recklessly self-destructive level she had dressed herself for Christian, in pale, delicate grey scattered with her usual minuscule white dots, the extravagant romance of the light chiffon a clever contrast to the sophistication of the seductively swathed bodice which left her shoulders bare. Oh, yes, she had known she looked her sexy best, she acknowledged bitterly, recalling how she had removed most of her jewellery because it distracted, contenting herself with a few pieces of silver, hoops in her ears and a slim bangle on one wrist.

But she had never played it down, she reminded herself defiantly. It had been a rebellious decision made years ago, and it had never endangered her or others before because she had always been able to cope kindly with the effect she had on men...

Men who left her unaffected...

Christian wasn't one.

Hence this mess. She had made it all by herself, Blythe accepted sardonically. She had been so smugly confident that she could deal with Christian to begin with, and then too self-indulgently greedy for some contact with him to ask Mr Lau to replace her and thus take herself safely out of his life.

And dear heaven, how was she ever going to extricate herself now?

'Please,' she began, soft voice strained as she swayed slightly.

'Yes!' Christian responded emphatically, and his mouth dropped to hers as if he were starving.

It was too much for Blythe. Desire had been a simmering, smouldering torment for too long. The fierce erotic pressure of his lips made it a raging conflagration. She clung to him, welcoming his mouth as it invaded hers, instant heat, like liquid fire, stabbing at her loins.

She loved this man, she realised all over again, somehow more shocked than she had been the first time. This man with whom it was folly to hope that she might find enduring happiness. What had she done to herself? What was she still doing to herself?

She needed to tear herself from the passion of his embrace, but at the same time she craved the ecstasy his hotly ravishing mouth was pledging, and she wound her arms possessively about him as if she could thus force from him the lifelong commitment she needed to stay her hungry heart between the brief periods of physical rapture which were all he could give her and which would never, ever be enough to satisfy this demanding love of hers.

Blythe moaned unhappily, savagely torn between the urge to yield to the compulsion of the moment and find transient joy, and the need to look to a future in which Christian would be gone from her.

That was the outrage. Just for a moment, her fingers were claws, biting angrily into him. Christian would go from her and she wouldn't be able to endure it. She could not bear to be one of many.

'God, Blythe,' Christian was gasping as he tore his mouth away from hers, and she felt the agonised clenching of his body against her. 'I know! It's bad, isn't it? I can't remember ever wanting like this before. We shouldn't have waited this long. Now it's happening too fast, unless we can slow it down, and I'm not sure if we can...are you? Do you ache for me, my darling? Is there a——'

'Christian...'

Her body stirred restlessly against the vibrant movement of his as his name came sighing helplessly from her sensitised lips, and he broke off to kiss her again.

She loved him, but at that moment she hated him too for what he was doing to her, arousing her, stoking the violent need that stormed in her, rendering her mindless, preventing her from finding a way to end this.

And if she did succeed in ending it, she would again be what she had been last time he had started to make love to her—a tease. He would hate her, despise her— and she would despise herself, because hadn't she, with her body's wild response to him, given him the right to expect to become her lover?

She tried, though, but her body wouldn't go limp this time; nor would her mouth still and her hands fall away from him. She was too involved, caught up in what he was doing to her, as much part of the havoc as he, her passion mounting in response to his, desire building intolerably.

The kissing was no longer enough and, half carrying her, Christian was moving her towards one of the lounge couches, lowering her to it and bending over her. Her breathing shallow and rapid, Blythe watched from beneath half-closed lids as, having found the zip of her dress, he slid the bodice downward and paused, catching his breath.

'You're lovely,' he breathed, and seemed slightly startled when she cried out softly as his hands touched the taut swell of her full breasts. 'And very, very sensitive, I think.'

The discovery seemed to cause him to put a check on his passion, although perspiration beaded his brow and his features were rigid as he began to draw delicate circles on the flawless creamy flesh. Closer and closer still, the lightly caressing fingers moved towards the proud dark nipples, but always avoiding them, and Blythe whimpered anxiously, her head thrown back in need, anticipation and even a little fear.

'Please!' she muttered urgently, and he searched her face quickly, his glance sweeping from the sensual shape of her mouth to her eyes, mere glittering slits beneath the languid eyelids.

The sharp sting of pleasure when finally his fingertips brushed those tight hard buds made her draw a harshly groaning breath.

'And your heart is going mad,' he teased, one hand slipping momentarily but returning immediately to cover the swollen aching flesh it had left.

He seemed to know the precise moment when her need for delicacy ended, his caressing hands becoming passionately possessive, fingers kneading, stroking and massaging, and Blythe's own fingers went impatiently to the buttons of his shirt.

'Yes,' Christian encouraged her jerkily. 'Do it for me, Blythe... Show me what you do.'

Her hands swept his chest, fingers skimming flat hard nipples and tangling in soft dark hair, and small shudders rippled through his body.

The excitement piercing her was unbearable. Touching him, being touched by him, was pleasure beyond belief.

'Your mouth,' Blythe begged feverishly, imagining its warmth would soothe the lovely, terrible torment of his fingers.

Christian laughed unevenly. 'You know exactly what you want, don't you? Yes.'

Instead of soothing, his mouth incited, taking voluptuous possession of one pulsing red nipple, and Blythe went wild as pang after pang of exquisite pleasure went shafting through her whole being. A long whispering cry came from her as the heat pooled in her womanhood became an empty burning ache, and she arched, hips lifting frantically to the power of his loins, while her hands came to his head, fingers tearing at his hair.

Christian groaned against her breast, his lower body surging against hers in a thrusting movement, and she felt a thrill of shock at the raw virility of the explicitly potent demand.

He raised his head, his hips now moving ceaselessly and urgently against her.

'Slow down if you can, sweetheart,' he urged tautly. 'We're going too fast.'

'I can't!'

Perspiration filmed her upper body and her head moved frenziedly from side to side until her lips encountered his flesh and she began kissing him, his chest and throat and shoulders, desperate, softly biting little kisses, tasting his skin, nipping at his shoulder.

'My God, are you always like this?' Christian sounded simultaneously awed and indulgent as the hot, hungrily devouring kisses continued. 'A small, sexy savage?'

It was all right for him, Blythe thought resentfully. He was used to this——

Something died in her. Her lips stilled against the warmth of his shoulder and her arms loosened their hold on him.

Christian didn't notice.

'Take it easy, sweetest,' he was continuing in that seductively caressing voice that melted her bones, although there was a slight raggedness to it now. 'It's going to happen, I promise you . . . But I suggest that if you want the comfort of a bed then we should make a move now or we're not going to make it at all, and couches are restrictive.'

He should know. It was a bitter little thought. Blythe glanced up at his face quickly and a silent cry seemed to fill her heart. She loved him so much! She didn't want to be just another affair. She wanted to be his one and only. She had to be! It was that or nothing——

Only there was no way she could deny him now when his face was tight and dark with desire and his vital body jerked and quivered powerfully against hers.

She could only turn him off—or scare him off.

But how?

'Christian,' she began urgently.

'It's all right,' he soothed, although he was hardly calm himself. 'You're going to be mine—and I yours. It's something very special, isn't it? Unique, made in heaven. We belong...'

Then Blythe had it. Maggie Huang's moon-face drifted past her mind's eye. What sent a playboy running?

'Christian, are you sure you mean it?' She had never been coy in her life, and she didn't quite manage it now either, but it did emerge suitably breathless, mainly because his hand was cupping a breast, fingers gently squeezing. 'Then don't you want to... But no, I suppose there's no need for us to be married first.'

Had the situation been only slightly different, she would have collapsed in a fit of giggles. Christian's hand dropped away from her breast, his body went dead still and his eyes narrowed. The only thing missing was a shocked pallor.

'What did you say?'

Blythe looked down—and wished she hadn't, because her breasts provided shocking evidence of the tumult rioting in her body.

'Oh...well, I suppose I misunderstood.' She bit her lower lip delicately. 'When you said... Oh, well, never mind, let's forget it. Where were we? I'm sorry, Christian. Carry on.'

'Not at all.' Christian had never sounded so courteous. 'Please excuse me a minute, Blythe?'

Abruptly she was free, with the couch to herself as he left the room.

Perhaps he had gone to summon help, she reflected hysterically.

She sobered. This was the breathing space she needed. She hitched up the bodice of her dress and slid the zip up before finger-combing her curls. She wasn't letting Christian get near her again. She lost her mind when he did, or at least lost sight of herself and her needs. Tomorrow she would ask Mr Lau to find another assistant for Christian.

It was more than a minute before he returned, his shirt rebuttoned.

'Sorry about that,' he apologised politely, sitting down beside her. 'And I hope you'll forgive the other lapse as well. I got carried away. You're absolutely right—we ought to wait until our wedding night. I feel like doing something truly conventional for a change, don't you? But let's talk about our wedding.'

Blythe's jaw dropped, as his ought to have done several minutes ago. Then her face hardened and she hid her eyes, realising what had happened. Christian was calling her bluff. He had guessed that was what it was and it had appealed to something in his sense of humour, prompting him to play up to her.

There was only one thing to do, and that was call *his* bluff right back, making hers a sort of double bluff. He would soon be running.

She slanted him a gently malicious smile. 'Here or at home in England?'

'I think it will have to be here, since it will have to be soon—very soon.' Christian's glance dropped meaningfully to her body. 'And I haven't nearly finished going into all I came here to ascertain, but we'll make time for a proper honeymoon, however short, I promise you.'

He wasn't serious. He couldn't be! Confident of that if of nothing else, Blythe decided to play along.

'But I want my parents at my wedding. You'll just have to fly them out, Christian.' That was it, she realised triumphantly; the wealthy were always suspecting people of trying to milk them of their fortunes. 'They're saving for a trip to Alaska and I certainly can't afford to pay for them to come to Hong Kong.'

'I might even fly my own parents out, since I'm their only child. I shouldn't think they'll approve of you, but don't let it worry you,' Christian advised her blandly.

'I'll want a massive engagement ring,' she went on a trifle desperately.

'We'll choose you a rock tomorrow. What sort of stone do you like?' The light blue eyes gleamed with unholy enjoyment.

Blythe pouted. 'I've never really been into jewels, just metals. I suppose a plain old diamond will do.'

'My darling, there's nothing plain about a diamond,' he retorted drily. 'But it's a good choice. A diamond says and means whatever anyone wants it to, and it will suit you.'

She drew a breath and rushed on, gabbling slightly, 'And then I've always dreamed of a big engagement party, and since I've been in Hong Kong I've imagined booking out the *Pearl of the Orient*. Think of it, cruising about Victoria Harbour, dining and dancing, watching the planes touch down on the runway at Kai-Tak, all lit up and stretching out into the sea.'

'Who would have dreamed you were such a romantic?' he drawled. 'We'll even invite Ward Smith.'

'And Trish Crewe, I suppose?' she said waspishly.

Oh lord, she was starting to believe in this!

'But not Vicky Short.'

Obviously his bank balance wasn't a major concern. She decided to intimidate him with domesticity.

'I hope someone gives us a wok as a wedding present. Mine is so old, and I do some really good stir-fries. There's a recipe using chicken and litchis that I can't wait to try on you.'

'Home cooking yet!' gloated Christian. 'Blythe, is there no end to your talents? You should have said. We could have dispensed with tonight's caterers.'

She would just have to shame him out of this, then. Blythe looked him straight in the eye.

'I want to get married in church.'

'We'll find out how these things are done in Hong Kong tomorrow morning. As it's still on lease, it shouldn't prove too complicated.' He paused, flashing her a knowledgeable smile. 'Church, yes. D'you think Rollo Crewe would be my best man? And then we'll have to decide on a venue for the reception. I suppose Lau will want to make a speech.'

This wasn't real. It wasn't really going to happen, Blythe told herself hysterically. In another moment he would get cold feet and back down.

'He'll probably warn me that I'm making a terrible mistake,' she predicted.

'There are people who'll tell me the same.' Christian waited a moment. 'What about our honeymoon? That's what's really on my mind. The rest is all just a list of necessary evils leading up to it. Where shall we go?'

She went for his pocket again.

'Pattaya,' she decided.

'Oh, definitely a romantic choice!'

'How do you know I'm not marrying you for your money?' she asked baldly.

'Because you're marrying me for my body.' He laughed. 'And for the novelty of it because, I imagine, you're tired of the sort of relationships you've been having, they've begun to pall, and you want to try something new. I'm the same. I'm ashamed to remember that I thought you didn't present any sort of challenge. This is the biggest challenge of all. It could be a great adventure. For sure it will be fun.'

Was that it? Her bluff had appealed to him as a challenge, sufficiently unusual to whet his jaded appetite. Oh, he knew it was a bluff, but he was probably amusing himself, waiting to see how worried he could get her, wondering how soon she would panic and back down.

Damn it, she wouldn't back down, but oh, dear heaven, what had she done? How far did they have to go?

Of course, sooner or later Christian was going to have to admit that he was joking, but until then she was going to have to play her part in this latest game, unless she wanted to give him the satisfaction of being the first to panic.

To test how far he was prepared to go, she asked, 'What about my job?'

'Unfortunately the general geographical disposition of Ballantine Holdings prevents my basing myself permanently in Hong Kong, but you might as well stay with Triple A until I've finished my work here.' He frowned slightly. 'Will you mind very much when the time comes to leave? Or perhaps you'd prefer not to work at all?'

'No, not that.' Blythe thought she could probably frighten him into abandoning the game right now by making some reference to giving up work when they started a family, but complex emotion held her silent on that particular subject. 'I enjoy working.'

'Or were you referring specifically to your temporary appointment as my assistant?'

'The question included that. What about it?'

Christian looked thoughtful and she felt an odd *frisson* of apprehension.

'There are various theories as to the wisdom of working with someone with whom you're also involved on a personal level.' He shrugged. 'On the whole, I think I'd like the arrangement to continue. I enjoy your company and you're efficient, even if you are the most distracting and least respectful assistant I've ever had.

Or are you going to turn all docile and dutiful, now that you've successfully snared me?'

That last phrase gave rise to an inexplicable feeling of guilt, almost as if that really was what she had done—which was ridiculous! This wasn't real; there wasn't really going to be a wedding.

'Don't sound so vain,' she admonished him tartly. 'You're not such a great prize.'

'Except that you want me—rather desperately, I would have said,' he taunted softly.

'Isn't it mutual?' she wondered innocently.

Christian laughed appreciatively. 'You know the answer to that, lady.'

'But do I?' She pouted a little. 'Perhaps I'm making a terrible mistake. It seems to me that a quite remarkable cooling process has taken place. Not so very long ago, you were talking about heading for the bedroom, and pronto; now you're content to wait until we're married.'

'Because I *can* wait, now that I know it's going to happen,' he retorted, scorching her with a blazingly triumphant smile. 'Before, when I wasn't one hundred per cent sure, in view of your tendency to tease, I wanted to snatch, like a greedy youth.'

'But now you are sure.' Blythe made her smile enigmatic.

'Absolutely—and if you try to back out, I'll sue you for breach of promise,' he warned her lightly.

Had she actually made any promises? Blythe couldn't be sure.

'Likewise, Christian,' she snapped, almost meaning it—almost believing in all this.

'As I believe I commented earlier, you know exactly what you want. So do I. Such perfect accord bodes well for the future.' Christian was outrageously complacent.

'Shall we open a bottle of champagne and celebrate our contract?'

'I'm not so sure that there's anything to celebrate.' Blythe stood up swiftly. 'But it will have to wait. I have to drive myself home, remember?'

She watched warily as he rose gracefully. If he still meant to take her to bed tonight, he would hastily dismantle the wild fantasy they had constructed right here and now.

'Of course, your safety must come first.' The devoted tone was slightly overdone, she considered. 'You don't always use your car, though, do you? Perhaps in future I should fetch you and take you home.'

'You'd probably go over your mileage limit if we started such an arrangement,' she returned prosaically, referring to measures which had been imposed in an effort to reduce Hong Kong's traffic. 'What with the subway trains, ferries, buses, mini-buses, taxis and the tram, I can manage quite easily.'

Christian was grinning at her offhand manner. 'And you have no intention of allowing me to pamper you? I wasn't planning on it, darling.'

'I suppose you expect me to do the pampering?' she challenged as they left the lounge.

'Would you?'

'No.'

'I thought not.' He opened the front door for her. 'Oh, we're going to have a very interesting marriage, Blythe.'

If they were going to have a marriage at all, she amended silently and sceptically. At her car, she turned and risked a look at his face, but it provided no clues.

'Goodnight, darling,' he said, reaching for her.

Blythe put a hand flat against his chest, keeping him literally and precisely at arm's length. So he was prepared to extend this joke that had been hers to begin with but which now seemed to be very much on her.

'If my safety comes first, perhaps you'd better not kiss me...darling,' she added mockingly. 'After all, didn't you once claim that you went to my head like wine?'

'And you're admitting it at last?'

'It would be pointless to deny it,' she responded drily, and Christian laughed and kissed her anyway, a long, lazy, devastating kiss that made Blythe tremble, mewling softly with pleasure and desire, all resistance melted so that it was as well that he retained control for both of them.

It took her a while to recover, and even then there was no emotional or mental relief for her as she drove home, her mind churning as she reviewed this latest development.

Once again, she was solely responsible for her predicament. She had mentioned marriage, thinking it would frighten Christian into leaving her alone...

While her greatest defence, the one thing that was guaranteed to have scared him, had gone unused.

So she had probably been fooling herself all along. She didn't want to frighten Christian out of her life.

She did want to marry him.

CHAPTER SEVEN

'WHAT went wrong?' Maggie Huang asked Blythe when the news broke.

'He called my bluff.' Blythe laughed a little shakily. 'And your question makes a refreshing change, Mags. All the other girls have been asking me what went right, and how I did it, until I feel sick.'

'They're awed and envious,' Maggie excused them, glancing questioningly at the door to Christian's office. 'Is he in?'

'No, he's with Mr Lau.'

'After all, in their eyes you've pulled off an impressive coup,' Maggie continued teasingly. 'The great international playboy—netted!'

'Don't you start!' Blythe groaned. 'I feel terrible.'

'Come on, girl, you can get out of it,' Maggie offered bracingly.

'But I don't want to!' Blythe wailed and, into Maggie's stunned silence, added quietly, 'I love him.'

'Oh.'

'Oh.' Blythe laughed, but the sound had a frantic edge to it. 'That's why I feel so awful when I hear all you people. So guilty! Because in a way I have—netted him, to employ your gross description. Trapped him. Oh, not in any of the more common ways, like saying I was pregnant, or the classic bribe, telling him he could only have me if he married me first. But I raised the subject. I believed I was trying to scare him off, but there was something else I could have used, much more effectively, so I think that subconsciously I must have hoped he'd

118

react just the way he did. He knew I wasn't serious when I pretended to assume he was talking marriage, but he decided to play along, I suppose because he's bored and it amused him. So here we are, each waiting for the other to back down and confess that it was all just a joke. I suppose Christian will be forced to in the end, because I won't, and then I'll have to accept it ... But, Maggie, if he's cussed enough to go through with it, I'm going to let him. I won't stop it. The marriage ceremony, our vows, may mean nothing to him, but it will give me a slight advantage over all the other women in his life. I won't be just another affair—that was what I couldn't accept. I'll be his wife!'

'Oh, Blythe.' Maggie shook her glossy head. 'Oh, Blythe! I'm speechless. You know exactly what you want, don't you?'

'Christian said that too.' Blythe paused and a surprised expression crept into her face. 'You're right, I do. I want him. I know how I must sound, and half the time I'm desperately ashamed of myself. It's as if falling in love has turned me into a monster, or one of those man-chomping bitches in the late-night black-and-whites on television.'

'But Christian Ballantine hardly conforms to the gentlemanly wimps who allow themselves to be chomped because that's what their code of honour dictates,' Maggie retorted, her dark Oriental eyes slitted by a grin of pure enjoyment.

'Thank you for those words of comfort and encouragement.' Blythe was gloomily sarcastic.

'What else can I say, since the last piece of advice I gave you has led you so sadly astray?' Maggie was giggling openly by now. 'And what, tell me, does our Mr Lau think of it all?'

'Marriage equals respectability in his book, so what can he think? He didn't actually say so, but I got the impression that he thought if I could wring a proposal from the notorious Ballantine then I was eminently capable of looking after myself and in no need of guidance from him.' Blythe grimaced. 'He was more concerned about Miss Vicky Short's reaction to the news and suggested that it would be tactful if I kept well away from her.'

'One of his little darlings. Yes, I've heard that she chewed bravely at a trembling lip, lost the battle and turned on the waterworks.' Maggie was unsympathetic. 'The girl's a neurotic, clinging to an impossible dream... But I imagine it's infuriating—galling—to see you turning the dream into reality for yourself.'

'It will probably turn out to be a nightmare. I suppose you'll be there to laugh at me at our official engagement party on the *Pearl*?'

'I wouldn't miss it.'

'And our wedding, if it actually takes place?' Blythe hesitated briefly. 'I've been thinking. You'd better be my bridesmaid, since you gave me the idea that led to this whole farce. It's a horrible job, I'm sure, so you deserve it. Plus, you're my friend. Will you do it?'

'Are you sure? Of course, you haven't got a sister. What about cousins?' queried Maggie.

'Those I've got have always suspected their husbands and boyfriends of wanting to run off with me, and blamed me for it. Anyway, they're all in England and couldn't make it out here at such short notice.' Blythe smiled. 'I do want you, Maggie—if this wedding really happens.'

'Then thank you.' Maggie paused and laughed. 'I suppose I have to make amends somehow.'

'Oh, dear, I keep falling into the trap of believing that this marriage is really going to take place,' Blythe added savagely. 'It isn't, of course, however much I may want it to. I suppose I've grown used to the idea simply through thinking about it so much.'

'If you want it so badly, it may well happen,' Maggie offered encouragingly. 'I'll stand by anyway.'

Blythe shook her head slightly and indicated the diamond blazing on her left hand.

'Christian Ballantine can afford expensive jokes, and I'm not sure how far he'll take this one, but surely he has to stop short of the actual wedding? Maggie,' Blythe's voice dropped, 'there have been telephone calls to both sets of parents and their flights to Hong Kong are booked and paid for; so is the *Pearl of the Orient* for the engagement party, the church for the wedding and a hotel's function-room for the reception.'

'If it's a charade, it's an elaborate one,' Maggie commented drily. 'It sounds to me as if he intends the wedding to take place, Blythe.'

'But how can he? Look at it logically, Maggie. He can't have any intention of actually marrying me! He's just obstinately determined to panic me into being the one to back down, but he'll have to come to his senses when he realises that I'm not going to.'

Blythe knew that, and yet she went on making practical preparations for marriage, and in far more important areas than merely choosing her bridesmaid. She had been to see her doctor, for one thing. The chances of this mythical projected marriage becoming reality were slender, and if it did, the chances of its working were even slimmer, she suspected sadly, since Christian was incapable of loving, while she would demand the fidelity only love could guarantee. To add an innocent baby to the situation would be criminally irresponsible.

Sighing after Maggie had left, she lifted the receiver of the telephone on her desk, but replaced it slowly as Christian walked in, her smile a little tense as he shot her an enquiring glance.

'I was going to ring Ward Smith,' she told him candidly. 'He left a message earlier.'

'The pilot,' he remembered curtly.

Blythe drew a breath. Christian must not be given any excuses for accusing her of failing to take their engagement seriously and getting out of it that way; thus she was determined to do everything by the book.

'Would you mind if I had lunch with him today, assuming that he's free?' she asked composedly. 'I ought to explain to him that I can't go out with him any more, now that I'm engaged, and I'd rather not do it over the telephone.'

'A coward's way,' Christian agreed abruptly. 'And since you're not one, I won't offer to do it for you either, but would you like me to be there?'

'No, thank you. You'll probably meet him at the party or the wedding, if he's in town for either,' she added.

'Will his pride let him attend after you've dumped him? It might be tactless, adding insult to injury, to invite him,' Christian cautioned her. 'But you know him, I don't. Is it going to be a difficult thing for you to do, telling him that there's someone else?'

Blythe shook her head. 'No, not difficult—for either of us.'

'It had burnt itself out?' he questioned her.

'It never burnt,' she returned simply, and saw his sceptical look. 'What about you, Christian? Have you dealt with all the attachments at home and in the States?'

He smiled. 'There weren't any, and haven't been for some time. That's why I arrived solo.'

It was Blythe's turn to be disbelieving. 'How do you handle the end of a relationship? I think I see you instructing your permanent assistant to dispatch a token bauble and her ringing up a jeweller and ordering "the usual". What's she like, by the way, or does she keep having to be changed?'

'She's a regal married lady in her late forties whose only passion, other than her husband, presumably, is Verdi. She doesn't approve of me.' Christian's tone hardened as he added, 'Are you going to be a possessive wife, Blythe?'

'Yes, I think I am,' she admitted, sighing inwardly because it was that aspect of her love which might rob them of any chance they had of making their crazy marriage work—if it even took place.

'Then I shall have the right to be a possessive husband,' Christian warned her, sounding uncharacteristically grim. 'I shall be suspicious and jealous of every man you look at, and you can expect an interrogation when you return from your lunch with Smith this afternoon.'

It was a part he was playing, whereas her possessiveness and uncertainty were all too real, Blythe acknowledged bleakly. If he had only fallen in love with her as she had with him, she knew she would not have felt them. The women in his past would cease to matter, and love would ensure that she was the only woman in his future.

Not even at lunch could she avoid reminders of Christian's reputation.

'I've heard about Christian Ballantine,' Ward Smith, a softly spoken Australian, said in the restaurant at which they met. 'This is going to surprise a lot of people because he's had quite a reputation. And yet it's not so surprising in one sense. It was always going to take a girl like you, if anyone, to change his ways, convert him to the idea of marriage. You're someone very special. Are you happy?'

'Absolutely,' Blythe assured him, less honest than she had been with Maggie. 'Oh, I know it won't be easy, that I'll have to work at it, because Christian is used to variety, of course.'

'You'll do it.' Ward was confident, and the open sincerity in his pleasant freckled face told her it was more than mere gallantry. 'But I have to tell you that the image of you that I've been cherishing is now shattered. I had this fantasy that no man would ever win you because you're so special that it would be unfair to all the others in the world if you chose just one.'

Blythe laughed. 'Fantasy is right. I've always wanted to marry, although Christian turned out to be a surprise.'

'Anyway, I wish you both all the joy there is. Your engagement party is out, unfortunately, but I'll try like hell to be here for your wedding,' he promised her.

'What about your own wedding?' she asked gently. 'Any progress?'

'A little, but as always, it's painfully slow. The others don't notice it at all really, except for her therapists, but because of my absences I do see slight changes every time I get back to Sydney, thank heaven. Otherwise I'd have given up hope with the rest of them.'

Blythe was still reflecting on the impartial way in which tragedy overtook the nicest people when she got back to the office.

'Was it bad?' asked Christian, entering her office within a minute of her return and noticing her sombrely thoughtful face. 'Worse than you anticipated?'

'Not at all,' she told him.

'It's too late for regrets, Blythe,' he warned harshly, startling her.

'Too early for them, you mean,' she quipped. 'We're not married yet.'

'You think we're going to repent at leisure?'

'Haven't you considered the possibility?'

'I imagine anyone who's getting married does that, unless they're the most obstinate of optimists,' Christian responded cynically. 'Without being one, I nevertheless think the likelihood of our repenting is somewhat reduced by the fact that we're both fairly sophisticated realists at a stage in our lives when we're ready to try something new. If we were both still enjoying our freedom to the full, or were so young as not to have tasted it properly yet, then there'd be more chance of both regrets and resentment.'

'I'm only twenty-three,' Blythe reminded him sharply.

'A highly sophisticated twenty-three, but also young enough to adapt.' He paused. 'How did Smith take your news?'

'He wished us both happiness.'

'How civilised!' Christian inserted sardonically.

'He can't make the party, but he's going to try to be at our wedding,' Blythe concluded.

'I can hardly wait,' he drawled. 'Is he the only ex with whom I'm to be confronted, or have you invited others?'

'The only one.' She slanted him a malicious little smile. 'And you, Christian? Is it the claws or the knives that will be out? Do I protect my eyes or watch my back—or throw myself in front of *you* to save you from some woman deranged with grief?'

'Why should she be deranged with grief? I'm only getting married, not buried.'

There was a glint in his eyes that made Blythe wonder if he was already beginning to find her jealousy a trial. Or perhaps he was warning her that he didn't intend to let marriage restrict him, once he tired of her.

Oh, but they weren't really going to get married...were they?

'There are some people who'd regard the two as one and the same thing,' she remarked, aware that he himself was probably one.

He laughed, relaxing. 'Would you really do that, Blythe? Defend me from some vengeful harpy—as you seem to imagine all the women in my life must be, goodness knows why?'

Because she was judging them by herself and she knew she wouldn't be a good loser if Christian was her lover and she lost him.

Blythe looked at him through the screen of her eyelashes. 'I might. I don't want a...damaged husband.'

'You only want me for my body,' Christian mourned facetiously.

'How did you guess?' she snapped, his pretended hurt too like a satirical send-up of her own real pain to amuse, and she saw his face harden.

'It's not a question of guessing. But to return to the central topic, I can assure you that none of the women I've ever been involved with would make an exhibition of herself in the way you're imagining. They're all as capable of civilised behaviour as your Captain Smith.' Christian's smile taunted her.

'Oh, I know Trish is,' she allowed.

'All of them—you should know that. You know my preference. Unlike the Vicky Short types with their tiny innocent minds full of powder-puff romance, that kind of woman doesn't embarrass herself or others by wearing her heart on her sleeve.'

'And Vicky and her *type* aren't on your guest list or mine.'

'Nor, to be honest, are the other kind, since Hong Kong hasn't really been one of my...hunting-grounds.'

'There's Trish,' she pointed out caustically.

Christian's face tightened again and he said bitingly, 'Do you really have a right to take this attitude, Blythe? We can't unwrite our personal histories. There've been women in my life, and men in yours.'

Fright and guilt gripped her, but resentment was greater, simply because he couldn't give her the love that would cancel out all her insecurity.

Blythe didn't think. She simply let temper take her, picking up the small pewter vase on her desk and hurling it at him.

'Your history is a damn sight longer than mine!'

It missed him by feet, but she saw his own famous temper flame in the blue eyes and he actually looked around for something to throw back at her.

Then suddenly he was laughing, his dark face lit with sheer, wicked delight.

'Ah, Blythe! All that superior talk about your parents and their excesses, but in the end you're their daughter and just like them! Oh, yes, I thought we were going to have a fascinating marriage, and now I know that it's not only in the throes of passion that you can lose control, I'm sure of it.' He examined her face amusedly. 'But not even losing your temper can bring a flush to that lovely skin. What about lovemaking? We haven't gone very far in that department yet, have we? Do you turn pink with excitement when you get as far as bed?'

'How should I know?' she flared incautiously, still furious.

'Of course, I was forgetting. No mirror on your bedroom ceiling, and perhaps your lovers have been left too spent and breathless to tell you,' he finished tauntingly.

'Will you get out of here?' she demanded, thumping a fist on her desk.

'I will, for now, but once we're married, my darling Blythe, we'll finish our fights—in bed.' Christian stooped gracefully to pick the vase up and place it on her desk. 'Lucky it was empty.'

It took Blythe a while to calm down, even left to herself. She had never lost her temper like that before, but then she had never loved before. Ruefully, she accepted that she probably was like her parents. It was only with each other that they lost their tempers, and they did love each other, quite unabashedly. Now Christian had unlocked the hereditary trait in her.

She was suffering from pre-wedding nerves, she tried to tell herself, and smiled forlornly. Had any bride-to-be ever viewed her approaching nuptials with as much uncertainty as she, not even sure if her prospective groom actually intended the marriage to take place?

Additionally, a mixture of fear and guilt was plaguing her by now. She knew she was cheating Christian, in so many ways. She meant to marry him if he didn't back down before the ceremony, and yet there were truths he didn't know which, if he did, would cause him to cancel the wedding instantly—truths which would send him running from her in horror, and not the least of these was the stark fact of her love for him. His open scorn of Vicky Short was evidence of that.

She still wasn't convinced that Christian was serious when they officially celebrated their engagement two nights later, in the below-deck salon of the *Pearl of the Orient* with its immense windows especially designed to offer stupendous views of the city and Kai-Tak's famous heart-stopping runway.

'So you pulled it off,' Trish Crewe congratulated her, drawing her aside while Christian was talking to Rollo. 'I wasn't sure if you would, but I thought you might have a better chance than most, simply because you're so unusual.'

She was unusual herself, Blythe reflected, giving her a thoughtful look, and despite the outré style she adopted, tonight's dress another so-called tartan, lavender and black checks with the thin lines running through them a pale tangerine, she remained very, very lovely.

'You knew how it was and would be before I did myself,' Blythe realised quietly, giving her a small, contained smile.

'Oh, yes, I looked at you and listened to you, and knew you wouldn't settle for less, a compromise, even if it meant . . . setting a trap. Have you—— No, that's a personal question. But does he know yet, Blythe?'

'That I tricked him?'

'No, the other.' Trish looked into all that Blythe would permit her to see of her eyes and shrugged. 'You're cheating him.'

But he need never necessarily know. The thought was like a defiant shout in Blythe's mind.

'But why do you suppose he's marrying me, Trish?' she asked a little bitterly. 'He's cheating me too.'

'Is he? I wouldn't know, because he hasn't told me,' Trish returned coolly, her Nordic grey gaze grown slightly inimical.

Blythe's eyelids lifted slowly and they exchanged a direct, assessing look.

'It's a game to him, but you could stop it any time by telling him what you . . . think you know,' Blythe ventured softly, her eyes dropping warily again to hide a surge of hostility, but she thought Trish had seen it.

'Oh, yes.' Trish also spoke softly after a pause of several seconds. 'You might be right. One way or another, he's cheating you . . . Why should I want to stop it, tell me? The truth is that I'd rather be married to a balding fifty-year-old ex-war-junkie with a wrecked liver who once nearly let himself die of despair and cynicism than to Christian Ballantine. I pity you, Blythe, not because he's a difficult man but because the fact that the two of you are starting out cheating each other doesn't say much for your chances.'

'Are you girls tearing us to shreds again?' asked Rollo as he and Christian joined them.

'Rollo thinks I'm a brave man,' Christian claimed outrageously.

'Well, it took courage to marry Trish,' Rollo asserted, and spoilt the sardonic effect by adding softly, 'On both our parts.'

'But I have to disillusion you,' Christian continued, wickedly suave as he slid an arm about Blythe's slender waist. 'There was no choice between courage and cowardice in this case. The lady gave me none. She hooked me, played me and landed me.'

'Did you struggle?' Blythe retorted gently, grappling with the fluttery inward sensation his touch never failed to induce.

'Hardly at all, except to begin with,' he admitted blandly. 'It was all too enjoyable.'

'Perhaps it took courage for Blythe to go angling, Christian,' Trish suggested, and Blythe tensed slightly, but mercifully Trish refrained from elaborating.

'Did it, darling?' Christian enquired, his arm tightening about her.

'But look what I got!' Loving him, hating him, she sent him a flirtatious upward half-glance.

'I never thought of complacency as an attractive trait, and look at me now—I'm marrying it,' Christian commented, apparently humorously, and Blythe wondered if the others detected the hard edge to his tone. 'It's something that struck me from the first where Blythe is concerned... And here she is, resplendent in her triumph. Red is such a victorious colour, isn't it?'

The design of Blythe's silk-chiffon dress was almost puritanically plain save for the naughtily enticing dip in the neckline that just revealed the creamy upper swell of her breasts. It needed to be, because the colour was a sumptuous, blazing red, offset by the neutrality of her colouring with the sole exception of her fiery lips and painted nails. Her eyeshadow comprised two smudgy streaks of smoky no-colour and her light brown curls with their subtle fairer glints had been pulled up on top of her head but were otherwise unadorned, while her only jewellery was her new engagement ring and the small studs in her ears.

'And why not?' she countered lightly. 'But do I hear resentment there, Christian? Perhaps you're starting to panic?'

'Blythe, I'm not even apprehensive,' he crushed the taunting little challenge.

But Trish's talk of cheating returned to her, nudging at her conscience, and she knew she had to offer him at least one chance to extricate himself before it was taken even further. Just one, though.

When she could do so without being overheard, she said, 'Christian, I want to talk to you ... alone ... and before Mr Lau starts proposing toasts.'

'Let's go up on deck, then.' Christian's glance skimmed her face and came to rest on her mouth. 'Then I can kiss that sultry siren's mouth. Have you done something to it? It looks like the entrance to a furnace and I'm having all sorts of wild and erotic fantasies.'

'This is serious,' Blythe reprimanded him as they headed for the stairs, aware of several people smiling to see them go, but aware too that there were others who watched enviously.

'Kissing can be serious,' he agreed.

She didn't respond, waiting until they were on deck, with the velvety summer night air caressing their skin, only the faintest of breezes coming up off the water, created by the *Pearl*'s movement as she plied her way about the harbour.

Then she said baldly, 'Do you want out?'

He knew what she meant. 'No, Blythe, I do not, and neither do you. Yes, I know how it started, that you weren't serious when you raised the idea and I took you up on it . . . But the prospect appealed to both of us at some fundamental level. It's something new. I'm not letting you go. I think you know by now that I can't.'

Blythe lowered her head, accepting it, too hungrily in love to be altruistic and attempt to argue him out of his determination by pointing out all the drawbacks that would work against such a marriage, not least the fact that he was marrying her for all the wrong, frivolous reasons.

Her heart ached with the weight of the love it bore, and there was a physical throbbing deep inside her as she looked up at him in the light which came from the two, Island and mainland, sides of the city.

'Trish said she pitied me,' she told him slowly.

'That was really friendly of her!'

But despite the sarcasm, he wasn't really perturbed or angered. He was so sure of her that resentment rose.

'She also said that she'd rather be married to Rollo than you,' she added deliberately.

'Of course she would,' he concurred drily. 'Haven't you realised? Perhaps the gorgeous exterior deceives. Trish has the soul of a social worker, or a reformer. All that charity work of hers, and consciousness-raising, the resettlement areas and refugees, isn't just something she does to justify her existence and because it's expected of someone in her privileged position. She needs to do good, change people's lives. Hence Rollo. She also just happens to have fallen in love with him, even more to her surprise than his... Why are we talking about these people?'

'You really know her very well, don't you?' Blythe taunted, not looking at him.

'Stop it, Blythe. Don't do this.' It was shot through with a silky threat. 'It's hypocrisy, and you have no right. Lord knows, I wish you——'

His voice had roughened towards the end and he broke off abruptly, leaving her frightened. He was already impatiently contemptuous of the insecurity she couldn't hide, and how much more irritated was he going to become in future if she couldn't succeed in suppressing it? And how horrified and furious was he going to be if he ever realised that it existed because she loved him? At present, he presumably put it down to a feminine version of the sexual jealousy men were reputed to experience even when their emotions weren't involved— just as she herself had tried to attribute it to the same thing before she had accepted that she loved him.

'Prove it's unjustified,' she quipped quickly, intent on confirming his belief. 'Right now! Kiss me at once!'

He relaxed, laughing softly as she reached for him. 'I warn you, once started, I may not be able to stop.'

Their mouths met, molten with passion, as Blythe melted into his arms. The desire that never truly slept leapt once more to full frenzied life as she yielded herself to the hotly erotic claims of his mouth. She could feel her breasts grow heavily full and sensitive, and a sweet, shuddery sensation assailed the pit of her stomach.

Like this, surrendered to the physical aspect of her love, most doubts were diminished, because here there was full reciprocation. Christian's arms tightened convulsively about her and a tremor ripped through his hard, lean body as she drew him more deeply into the moist heat of her mouth.

She moaned softly and continuously, her hands tangling in his dark hair, her achingly alert body frustrated by the suit he wore as she writhed against him. His hands slipped to her hips and buttocks, lifting her to him, and the fiery deliquescence deep within the cradle of her loins became an urgent, imperative summons as he moved explicitly against her and she felt his need.

'I'm going up in flames,' she whispered shakily as their mouths parted momentarily.

'What do you think is happening to me?' Christian retorted unevenly, his body curving to the shape of hers in another surgingly compulsive movement.

Then their mouths collided again, merging, and the raging ache between Blythe's thighs intensified, became intolerable and a torment. Christian's hips ground ceaselessly against her now, exacerbating the pounding emptiness within her, and she was arching, answering to his demand, all desire, needing him to fill that hollow agony with his body.

She made a murmuring sound of protest when he ended it, holding her away from him, his breathing as unsteady as hers.

'Oh, there's nothing I'd like more than to take you home with me right now and spend the rest of the night discovering all the secrets this passionate, perfect body holds for my delight.' He ran a light hand over her from shoulder to hip. 'Arousing the passion, and satisfying it, Blythe, as you'll satisfy mine, and seeing your eyes fly open in the shock of pleasure . . . I think we're going to achieve rare heights, don't you? But we have guests waiting for us down below, and a formal announcement to endure... And having waited this long, I think we should carry on with the traditional bit and tantalise ourselves in anticipation of our wedding night, but not anticipate it in fact. It's quite a novelty, isn't it, to be waiting, going through all this ceremony, the ritual of an engagement... Shall we go down and make it official?'

As she put her hand in the one he held out to her, Blythe looked up at him.

'Are we really going to be married, Christian?' she asked, allowing him to hear her doubt for once.

'We are. Don't worry, you're not going to go deprived for much longer.' He laughed a little harshly, an odd resentment coming through. 'Lord, Blythe, do you think I could deny myself?'

He wasn't backing down yet, then, and perhaps he wouldn't, even at the eleventh hour. She had given him his chance to withdraw, but there would be no more, Blythe decided. She meant to marry him. It was probably folly, but she no longer cared.

She would marry Christian. She reaffirmed it mentally much later that evening, dancing in his arms, incandescent with desire and knowing that he wanted her too. In only this one area, the feeling was equal, and if physical attraction was love's most misleading facet and often nothing to do with love at all, at least it was something to build a flimsy hope on.

She knew Christian didn't love her, but she was still going to marry him.

CHAPTER EIGHT

BLYTHE looked at her husband and apprehension tightened her stomach.

She had married him. So what now? What next?

Beside her, Christian was relaxed and thoughtful as the Triple A airliner moved steadily through the Asian skies, but how would he look when they flew back this way in a week's time?

'What?' he enquired softly, turning his head and catching her glance.

'I was wondering how you'd look in a week's time,' she admitted, her gaze slipping away.

'What can you be planning to do to me?' His voice was a slow, warm caress.

'Wait and see,' she advised him in a whisper, risking a flirtatious upward glance. 'Have you enjoyed yourself so far?'

'More than I expected to,' Christian confessed. 'But it's incredible when you think of it all. The partying, the presentations, the people, all leading up to you and me standing there in church making a few promises. It was over so quickly. Other people's weddings always seem to take much longer.'

'Other people's weddings aren't so interesting.'

He laughed. 'Other people's weddings have other brides. I couldn't stop looking at you. That dress made you more stunning than ever.'

It had been a morning wedding, so Blythe had gone for simplicity, the bodice of her dress brief and uncluttered beneath a little fitted jacket, the skirt narrowing at the knee. She had worn white, but her individuality was expressed in the little polka-dotted half-veil that had screened her eyes, white on white, descending from the few fresh flowers she had worn in her hair just above her brow.

'You looked rather stunning yourself,' she returned lightly, and he smiled wickedly.

'Is that what robbed you of your voice?'

'What else?'

In fact, she had experienced a moment of utter panic in church, wondering what she was doing there, marrying a man who didn't love her and who still didn't really know her. The beliefs to which she had been raised plus a large dose of pure superstition had temporarily darkened her mind, convincing her that she was not merely courting disaster but probably damning herself.

Then she had glanced up at Christian again, feeling her heart clench with emotion, and her fears had dissolved. The vows he was making might mean anything or nothing to him, but hers meant everything.

'You look gorgeous now too,' he added, studying her vivid little saffron outfit appreciatively. 'Don't you want some more champagne?'

'I think I've had enough, on top of all I had at the reception. Maybe when we get to Pattaya.'

The reception had actually been a wedding breakfast.

'You won't need any then,' Christian promised her provocatively, eyes gleaming. 'But now? Are you sure?'

'Absolutely. I don't want a headache,' Blythe added mischievously, and he laughed.

'I'd cure it for you.' He paused. 'I'm sorry we can only take a week at present, especially as we've rushed into this so fast. Getting organised has probably been more hectic for you than for me, and in addition to that, it had to be a pretty high-profile wedding. It was expected of us if we were getting married at all, but it would have been even worse at home. One thing: once we get off this plane, we don't have to consider anyone but ourselves.'

'Oh, I haven't minded most of it.' It was the only wedding she would ever have, after all. 'And I'm already enjoying being the boss's wife, with the crew all treating me as if I were the Queen Bee. I've never flown first class before.'

'My wife!' There was a ring of astonished delight to his laughter. 'You really are!'

'I will be,' she corrected him significantly.

'Yes.' Christian picked up her left hand in his right and held his own left out beside it so that their new rings were on display. 'You will, and very soon. I'm just beginning to absorb it all. I have a wife, and parents-in-law. I like your parents, but I was disappointed that they didn't throw anything at each other in my presence.'

'They were on their best behaviour. They did have that quiet shouting match the other day when my mother thought my father was planning to go up to the Tiger Balm Gardens without her,' Blythe reminded him as he released her hand.

'He put the idea in her mind deliberately to provoke her. Do you know, Blythe, I thought they both seemed distinctly relieved when I told them you'd thrown a vase at me?' Christian went on amusedly.

She laughed. 'They think that sort of thing is the sign of a thriving, happy relationship. I don't need to tell you that they're thrilled with you, and the fact that we got married so soon after meeting each other has convinced them that I'm following in their footsteps. They had a real whirlwind romance. They got engaged the weekend they met and married one month later.'

'Unlike my parents, who remained soberly engaged for eighteen months because my father was just starting out in business then,' Christian said drily. 'I owe you an apology, Blythe. I didn't think they'd approve of you, but they melted like snow in a desert that evening we all got together at your place, and they even found they had something in common with your wacky parents, which didn't seem likely at first sight. I suspect the four of them are going to spend the few days that remain of their time in Hong Kong haunting one or other of the racecourses.'

'It all worked out beautifully,' Blythe agreed neutrally. 'A good omen for us.'

She would have liked to share with him her suspicion as to what had effected the thaw in his parents, because there had been a degree of frost to begin with. She had even inadvertently overheard Christian's father murmuring something about a 'femme fatale' to his wife. Then they had come over to her simplex for a barbecue in the courtyard and to be introduced to her parents, and she had seen them notice her teddy-bears and pictures, and turn, and look at her with new eyes. She had known what they were thinking—that someone who so loved the treasures of childhood would want to have children of her own. The relieved warmth in their attitude after that had convinced her: Christian's parents wanted grandchildren, were anxious for them, in fact.

But somehow babies were a subject she shrank from mentioning to Christian. It would frighten him, perhaps right out of their marriage, because he would begin to realise that he was in a trap.

He had fallen silent, and she let her mind drift over the events of the last few days—the arrival of their parents, hers wildly excited and gratified by the impetuosity of what their hitherto cautious daughter was about to do, the last-minute preparations for a fairly big wedding, and yesterday's party and presentation of a wedding present to which everyone at Triple A had contributed and from which, to Blythe's relief, Vicky Short had stayed away; she hadn't wanted any reminders at that late stage of how badly Christian could hurt a woman.

'Blythe?' Christian's gaze raked her face as she turned her head enquiringly. 'Talking of lengthy engagements...I had a few words with your Ward Smith at the reception. I assume you know that he has a lover in Sydney to whom he's been engaged for some years?'

'She was very badly injured in a road accident the night they got engaged, and she's having to re-learn everything, even the most basic skills, and speech. It was someone else's fault, not theirs, which is what makes it so cruel, especially as I know she must be as nice as Ward, and he's a lovely person,' Blythe added.

'And one of those rare men who's prepared to wait for her, forever if necessary, and moreover to be faithful while he's waiting. He didn't tell me, but I gathered that much.' Christian was silent a moment. 'He was never your lover, was he?'

'No.' One secret less, she thought.

'So what was in it for you?'

'We're friends.'

'Yes.' Accepting it, he smiled ironically. 'So you didn't do that to me. You didn't present me with even a solitary previous lover, gnashing his teeth or leaping up to halt the proceedings in church. You have a nice sense of propriety. You really have behaved with the utmost decorum ever since you engaged yourself to me.'

'I engaged myself to you? Didn't you have something to do with it as well, Christian? Oh yes, I did everything by the book. You see, I didn't want to lose you—give you an excuse to back out.' The flippancy hid her disturbance.

'I was never going to.' His countenance was unusually grim. 'So why did you let me think that Smith had been one of your lovers?'

'You and I were playing games with each other, Christian.' Blythe spread her hands, reflecting that he was still playing.

'Who won, incidentally?' His expression had cleared.

'I did, of course,' she claimed lightly, flashing her diamond.

'Strange—I thought I had. I feel as if I have.'

Nerves clenched in her stomach again.

'How long will you go on feeling that way?' she asked.

His face grew expressionless. 'I suspect the answer to that question is really up to you, Blythe.'

'But the game is over?'

'Yes, all the games are over. You do know why I married you, don't you?' he added with unusual urgency.

'Oh, yes.' She smiled vivaciously, hiding the sadness the knowledge occasioned, and Christian sighed slightly, probably relieved that she was under no illusions.

By the time she stood looking at the sumptuous double bed in the luxury honeymoon suite of their Pattaya hotel that night, Blythe had alternated between joyful excitement and fluttery apprehension scores, if not hundreds, of times in the last few hours.

At that moment, it was excitement. The place was a paradise, an idyllic setting for a dream honeymoon. It had still been light when they had arrived, a pale heat haze hung over the Gulf of Siam so that you seemed to see the tiny islands dotting the water through a filmy gauze. The hotel had a private beach as well as a pool, and they had gone down to the former for a brief swim in the warm, buoyant and gently heaving water before drinking Mai Tais at an outdoor bar prior to dining.

The bedroom's french window opened on to a balcony where Christian was at present, with an exotic flowering creeper trailing prettily over the railing and from which you could look out over the water, while inside, since this was Thailand, fresh orchids filled a couple of vases.

Blythe looked down at herself with a thoughtful little smile, half pleased now but wanting Christian's reaction to complete her pleasure, but he had already been outside when she had emerged from the bathroom. She had worn white for the wedding, but she hadn't been prepared to risk it on her wedding night. As her polka-dots seemed to amuse Christian, she had scoured Nathan Road's 'golden mile' of shops and side-arcades for this brief shift which now skimmed her body, the satin tinted palest peach and scattered at one-inch intervals with dots in the most delicate shade of grey that she had ever seen.

She looked at the turned-down bed curiously. Soft light spilled on to its immaculate smoothness. Soon she and Christian would occupy it, and become truly husband and wife, and she would know——

'Oh, Blythe!' There was a lilt of laughter in Christian's voice as he came inside, closing the french window behind him and then standing still, simply looking at her.

He didn't need to say more. Fully content now, she sent him a quick smile and one of her smoky half-glances.

'I suppose it's really still a bit too early to go to bed,' she ventured mischievously.

'It's not early at all.' His smile blazed out. 'In fact, in our case it's long, long overdue. Can you wait just a little longer? Give me ten minutes.'

'Five,' she bargained happily as he picked up his dark blue robe.

'Lady, the way I've always heard it, it's the groom who's supposed to be impatient,' he retorted.

'Oh, I didn't know. I've never been married before, so it's all new to me.'

'And me.' Christian's laughter caressed her. 'We're both absolute beginners at this, aren't we? I won't be long, Blythe.'

When he had gone, her confidence dipped slightly, deprived of the bolster of his open appreciation, and she looked round a little helplessly, wondering whether he expected to find her in bed when he returned, or draped seductively on the chaise-longue near the window.

As it happened, she was in the act of changing her mind and was halfway between the two when the bathroom door opened. She looked at Christian and he looked back at her, and she knew where he wanted her. She went to meet him, to welcome her husband, and he met her halfway, his arms sliding about her as hers were lifted to encircle his neck, her head thrown back, lips parted for his kiss, eyes half shut.

Passion exploded instantaneously, the impact jolting them both. Blythe had no control from the start, and she sensed that Christian wasn't far behind. Soon he was lowering her to the pristine freshness of the bed.

'Lovely as it is, shall we have this off?' he muttered urgently, and she let him remove the scrap of satin she had gone to so much trouble to find.

It would be all right, she assured herself as the ability to think restored itself for a moment. Oh, please God, it would be all right and she wouldn't disappoint him. She loved him, and he did want her.

Christian stilled, the breath held in his throat as she fell back against the pillows, letting him see her nakedness. A fierce fire burnt at the back of the blue eyes as they travelled from the slope of her shoulders and the thrust of her breasts to the evocatively welcoming circle of her pelvis, shaped to receive a man and hold his child, and the soft protective cloud that kept the secret at the fork of her body.

'Oh, but you're perfect,' he said slowly, his eyes returning to the blazing lure of her mouth and then her smouldering, slitted eyes.

Then, abruptly, he was shrugging out of his short robe, and her eyelids rose as she stared, unable to help herself, awed as she filled her vision with the magnificence of his proud dark body for the first time.

'I think I'm going to faint,' she murmured huskily when he moved towards her.

'You flatter me,' Christian retorted, the attempt at humour emerging jerkily as he bent over her.

The touch of his body along the length of hers, burning her, sent Blythe wild. The scorching heat of his flesh, the soft abrasiveness of his body-hair against her tenderly silken skin, his hardness against her yielding softness, all seemed so perfect, so right, so complementary, that she cried out in an excess of welcoming joy.

Too, there was the passion of his mouth on hers, in it, and then at her breasts, sensually suckling, and his hands moving all over her, and her hands on him, acquainting themselves with beautiful reality exceeding wildest fantasy.

But when Christian's hand sought the soft secret cleft of her body, something strange happened to Blythe, an instinctive, clenching resistance to the unknown. She loved him and wanted him so much that it was utterly unexpected, and she strove frantically to overcome it before he realised, but it was too late.

'What's wrong?' he asked, disconcerted, looking into her face.

'I...think I must be nervous. I'm not quite sure what to expect. I've never... No one has ever...touched me...'

Her voice died away as she saw his face. In terrible silence Christian withdrew from her, hesitating a moment before reaching for his robe and drawing it on. Then he sat on the edge of the bed, looking at her with murderous eyes, and she let her own stay open and fixed to his face, incapable of defence or dissemblement.

'I have understood you correctly, haven't I?' He spoke so harshly that she flinched.

'Yes.' The admission came sighing out of her, poignantly laden with regret and an aching despair. 'I didn't mean to tell you.'

'And hoped I wouldn't realise,' he surmised tautly, and his abrupt laugh was a shocking sound. 'If your body hadn't betrayed you now, it would have done so later.'

'I thought...it wouldn't. I wanted you, Christian,' she added emphatically. 'I still——'

'In heaven's name, why?' Temper exploded. 'And how? I'm not the only one who was deceived—I know that. I doubt if anyone in the world could look at you and guess the truth.'

'Trish did, but she listened,' Blythe muttered.

'And she didn't see fit to warn me,' he grated furiously.

'But you're right, most people think what you did,' she rushed on, suddenly under a nervous compulsion to explain herself. 'It's because of the way I look. It's been like that ever since I was a teenager. Mr Lau made the same mistake. That's why he chose me to be your assistant, because he thought I was experienced and therefore sophisticated enough to take care of myself and not get hurt like Vicky Short did. You'd asked for——'

'I know what I asked for,' Christian cut in contemptuously. 'I didn't get it, did I? I was deceived, and you let me, and everyone else, Lau and all the others, go on being deceived. But you didn't marry the others. What did you do that for, you lying little cheat? Was it some crusade you decided to wage on behalf of Vicky and the other innocents like her, to punish me for turning them away?'

'No!' The denial emerged sharp and distressed.

'Then why didn't you tell me the truth?'

'Because...' Blythe swallowed shakily. 'I think because I was afraid I'd lose you—that you'd lose interest in me. Because you'd rejected Vicky.'

Her glance slid away from his as she turned her head on the pillows, but hard fingers caught at her chin, forcing her to face him.

'Look at me,' he instructed her savagely and she obeyed despairingly. 'Why did you marry me?'

'I didn't want to be just another of your lovers.' Her voice cracked emotionally. 'I wanted to be something more than all the others.'

Because she was looking at him, she saw him accept it. He knew now that she loved him, and with the knowledge came everything she had feared, a compound of anger, disgust and resentment.

His mouth twisted as he released her chin, but he didn't speak for a while, simply sitting there looking at her, his eyes moving from her face and over her lovely nudity, but the only warmth his gaze contained was the heat of rage. Blythe's own eyes felt hot with tears and her heart was filled with a tight, hard anguish. The fact that he could look at her naked body without wanting to touch, without wanting her, said it all. One single small truth had wrought this change, stopped desire dead. She had lost him before she had even had him.

'Damn you, Blythe!' It was a raw, bitter condemnation, finally. 'Damn you to hell! Do you have any idea at all of what you've done to me, I wonder? You must know that I can't give you what you want—what you need.'

She had to stifle a cry of protesting denial at the brutally rending truth. She had always known it anyway, but hearing him actually admit it out loud hurt in a way she could never have imagined.

'Yes...' She hesitated. 'I suppose we could...get an annulment.'

'There's been enough cheating, and it would be.' Christian paused deliberately. 'Because we're going to consummate our marriage, Blythe, and see how long it lasts.'

'Christian?' She searched his face bewilderedly, finding an unrelenting resolution there.

'Later on we can talk divorce if you find you really can't endure the lack of emotional security,' he went on, once more discarding his robe with a single purposeful movement.

'I don't understand,' she whispered, unnerved by the ruthless intent that now marked his dark features.

'You should. This is, after all, the only way in which I can truly satisfy you. In bed.' His mirthless smile was a travesty. 'Of all your needs, and you require so much, too much of me, this is the one I can answer fully, the one aspect in which I don't fail you—and won't, and ironically that's partly because, unlike you, I do have some previous experience.'

It was a mercilessly cruel reminder, and Blythe understood that he was punishing her for loving him.

When he lay down beside her again, she surrendered herself to him, accepting his decision to make their marriage real, and even relieved by it. There was no reason to protest. He was giving her all she had expected of him, of their marriage. Nothing had changed except that she had his contempt and resentment to contend with now that he knew how completely she had cheated him.

As he had said, this was the sole aspect of her multi-faceted need that he was able to satisfy, and she was likewise capable of satisfying him, but since his need regarding her was limited to the purely physical, he was the one who would be wholly satisfied, she only partially so.

Just for a moment, Blythe wondered if she would be able to respond to Christian now, with the weight of so much unhappiness settling inexorably on her. For even less time, she flinched from the possibility that he might intend his lovemaking as a punishment, either emotional or physical.

Then their bodies touched and doubt disintegrated. It was going to be all right. In this, if in nothing else, they were equal in their need of each other. The truth about her, the trap into which she had led him, might repel Christian, but she did not.

'But there are so many ironies here,' he muttered, apparently as an addendum to what he had been saying before. 'Heaven and hell in the same package...'

He was kissing her, making a slow, sensual exploration of her mouth, gradually deepening, and Blythe wound herself about him with a feeling that she was dissolving within herself, her blood become liquid racing fire in her veins.

'Please,' she urged breathlessly as he ended the kiss abruptly.

'It's just occurred to me.' He grimaced sardonically. 'I assumed, along with everything else, that protecting yourself would be part of your natural way of life. Is there a possibility that——'

'No,' she interrupted him quietly, letting him see her eyes fully so that he would know he could trust her, and adding quietly, 'I wouldn't do that to you, Christian.'

'You've done enough as it is,' he agreed. 'But I wasn't thinking of myself.'

His mouth covered hers again before she could reply, and she arched to his powerfully stirring body. She sensed his restraint, even when his lips were transferred to the erect peak of one swollen breast, and the fingers that had caressed and teased it a moment before moved downward. With hands and mouth and the vibrant strength of his superbly made body, he continued the seduction, and Blythe responded wantonly, whispering his name brokenly, sighing and crying her pleasure.

The hands at her hips shook slightly, and Christian smiled wryly in answer to her enquiring look.

'I've never made love to a virgin before,' he confessed ruefully. 'I'm not sure if I know how, if I can—— I'm probably more nervous than you, Blythe.'

'Oh, Christian!' For the first time since she had shocked him with the truth, she smiled, very shakily, as her heart clenched in regret. 'I'm so sorry!'

'So am I,' he returned darkly. 'But it's too late now, so just forget everything beyond this if you can, my darling. Don't think—feel.'

'Can you?'

He looked at her for a moment.

'Yes!' he answered her emphatically, and a shudder racked him as he gathered her close in an urgent, compulsive movement. 'Oh, yes!'

This time she was so acutely sensitised, overwhelmed by the passion he had made it his task to arouse and then stoke, that she was free of apprehension and ready for him when his hand came to her upper thighs. She shifted to accommodate his gently cupping hand, gasping at the incredible, tenderly flooding sensation it induced.

Still she sensed the control he imposed on himself, waiting until he knew her desire rendered her invulnerable before unleashing the fullness of his own passion, his sweeping caresses and long searing kisses, given to every inch of her, inciting her to like, until he groaned beneath her lovingly possessive hands and the hotness of her seducing mouth.

They were wild in each other's arms, a throbbing, intolerable tension building, speeding their hearts and pulses and breathing. Then when Blythe was sobbing with desire and crying out, pleading with him to ease the agony in her loins and fill her unbearable emptiness, Christian moved between her thighs.

'All right?' he muttered harshly.

'Yes,' she groaned, and felt the heated hardness of him against her, waiting. 'Oh, yes, Christian, my darling, please!'

'Blythe?'

'Yes,' she said again, understanding what he wanted and letting him see her eyes.

The first stroke of his body in hers brought a shock of indescribable rapture, drawing a small cry from her that became a moan of urgent encouragement as she absorbed the sensation and sensed the greater rapture to come. Sure of his welcome, Christian proceeded, his thrusts deeper and sharper as he gathered her into his rhythm, and she went with him, rocking and arching beneath him, drawing him deeper still, while her hands kneaded and clutched at his sweat-filmed flesh.

Then the universe shattered about them and Blythe yielded herself to shuddering, extended ecstasy, gasping wild, joyous love-words as Christian too shuddered, with a harsh cry, in the spasm of his potent release, filling her with warmth.

Gradually everything came back together again and Blythe turned to Christian as he withdrew from her, searching his face while their breathing slowed. He looked back at her, his dark face unusually inscrutable, but after a few seconds he gave her a slight, reserved smile.

'Yes, you have that,' he offered slowly. '*We* have that. I can give you that.'

'And I you,' she countered defiantly.

'As new as you are to it, do you need me to tell you?' he retorted drily.

'No.' She smiled a little, and sighed involuntarily. 'I wish...'

'I wish too, Blythe,' he told her curtly. 'But it's futile, isn't it?'

She had no answer, and they were both silent, drifting into sleep after Christian had reached out and turned the light off.

They woke in darkness, seeking each other, more than once during that soft tropical night, and Blythe learnt all the ways of loving, ferocious and tender, and listened to Christian and learnt too to enhance every exquisite, erotic sensation as he did, with words, describing the sensations she was experiencing, questioning his, eloquent about what she was doing and what was being done to her.

Their energy fed on itself, it seemed, exhaustion unknown as passion flared yet again.

But when Blythe woke one last time to the light of day, Christian's face was closed to her in a way that it had never been before.

'I've embarrassed you as well as everything else, haven't I?' she accepted sadly.

'You demand so much.' There was a hard reluctance to his tone. 'More than I can give you, however much I may want to—and believe me, Blythe, I wish I could, I would to heaven that I could offer you everything you need from me. But I can't!'

It surprised her, but it didn't change anything, because the central truth remained. Christian couldn't love her.

She looked away from him for a little while, coming to terms with it. Then her chin firmed and she gave him a provocative little smile.

'It doesn't have to be a problem on our honeymoon, does it?'

He relaxed, laughter glinting in his eyes. 'No, it does not, and the demands you make in bed are another story entirely!'

'You're not exactly restrained yourself,' Blythe retorted, a tiny reminiscent smile flickering round her mouth which still bore witness to the demands she had answered, slightly swollen and with a new lushness to its redness.

'Are you sore?' he asked suddenly.

'A little,' she discovered, surprised, because there had been absolutely no pain the night before, and, seeing the odd regretful expression that crossed his face, she gave him another meltingly bewitching smile and moved so that she could rub her cheek against his warm, bare shoulder. 'And so I ought to be after all that!'

'Oh, Blythe!' Christian laughed softly with a combination of delight and rue.

They had an idyllic honeymoon. They flirted and laughed and made love, and in between they swam and snorkelled and ate seafood at waterfront restaurants in the town or on tiny islands to which they travelled by launch, and they viewed the sea-bed from a glass-bottomed boat, and even did some para-sailing, and attended one of Pattaya's famous and outrageous cabarets. Christian's suntan darkened beautifully, but Blythe merely turned a deeper shade of creamy brown.

It was the ultimate honeymoon, perfect in every respect save one, and it haunted Blythe. Her husband didn't love her.

CHAPTER NINE

'YOU look sexier than ever,' Christian commented, regarding Blythe with lazy appreciation as she joined him on the patio of the house on the Peak one evening a few days after their return to Hong Kong.

'It must be my satisfactory sex life,' she quipped lightly, placing the glass of Perrier water she had brought outside with her on the table and seating herself.

He laughed at the complacent little smile she gave him.

'Don't you ever wonder if you're tempting fate by being so pleased with yourself?'

'Frequently.' A tiny sigh escaped her. 'I think I've been doing it ever since I met you. I'm doing it now too, probably. But why shouldn't I be pleased with my sex life?'

After all, she didn't really have a love life.

Oh, yes, she had tempted fate. She had been so smugly confident that she could cope with him that fate had laughed and made her fall in love with him, and yet she supposed she had still gone on tempting fate in various ways ever since.

'When it's the only area in which I can truly—fully—satisfy you?' Christian prompted sardonically, as if he had caught the bitter little thought that had followed her challenge.

'Do you need to remind me?' she queried.

'I can't forget it, even if you want to. You know why.'

She ran a slightly brooding glance over the pile of personal mail Christian had brought out to the patio on their return from the office while she went to change into the ultra-feminine pale sea-green pants, pleated and loose but narrow at the ankles, which she was wearing with a matching, subtly revealing little bolero-type top.

She made herself smile carelessly. 'I just thought we should concentrate on what's positive, the things we have got going for us, that's all.'

'Yes.' His smile was rueful. 'And it's a lot, isn't it?'

But was it enough? Blythe's gaze returned to the pile of mail again. It had to be enough; she would make it enough, and she would start by not repeating the mistake she had made on their return from Thailand when the post awaiting them had included a card from one of Christian's former lovers. Initially, she had merely asked an idle question, but it had been her nervous awareness of Christian's instant defensiveness that had changed casual interest into curiosity.

'The affair ended years ago, and I never go back,' he had snapped when she ventured a second question.

'Just forward,' she responded tartly, and had seen the resentment blaze in his face for a moment before it became shuttered. 'You move on.'

That was what frightened her. He might never renew an old affair, but the number of women in his past was blatantly indicative of a taste for variety. He so clearly resented her love, and even if he didn't go back, he might begin to *look* back, with nostalgia, on all those sophisticates who he believed had so sensibly refrained from falling in love with him.

Now, following her glance, Christian pushed the pile of envelopes over towards her. 'Mostly more congratulations, probably, since they're addressed to both of us. Do you want to open them?'

'They'll all be from your friends, since they're for this address.'

'Our friends now,' he pointed out.

'You know so many people.'

For a moment he wore the defensive expression that had become all too familiar since their marriage.

'I suppose you mean women?'

'No, I don't, but if you want to make me jealous just carry on being so defensive about your past, Christian,' she snapped. 'I'm . . . It's difficult enough for me, knowing that——'

'Do you think it's easy for me?'

'I know it's not, but talking about it doesn't help.' Her eyes dropped to the pile of envelopes once more. 'They couldn't possibly all be from ex-lovers, anyway . . . could they? Not even you, Christian . . .'

Dark eyebrows rose sardonically. 'I'd really have to have been some kind of super-stud.'

'You're not?' Relieved by his change of mood, Blythe managed to slant him a mischievously incredulous look, and he laughed.

'That's the effect you have on me,' he allowed, but his voice cooled slightly as he added, 'Yes, I suppose I am being defensive—especially as I've already opened the only card I recognised as bearing an ex's hand-writing, but she was an ex-girlfriend, not an ex-lover, since we decided we didn't suit each other before things got that far.'

'But you still keep in touch?'

'Yes. I do a certain amount of business with the engineering firm she works for, and we get on well. Here.' He passed her the card he had opened.

Blythe glanced at it reluctantly. 'Just conventional good wishes.'

'Yes, absolutely innocent. It could never have been anything else.' His mouth twisted as she remained silent, determined not to ask the obvious question. 'So now you're wondering why I took the trouble to open it while you weren't around, aren't you?'

'Oh, I know why you did it, Christian,' she claimed, faintly bitter. 'Because even innocence can be misunderstood or misconstrued, especially by a jealous, suspicious mind.'

What he didn't seem to realise was that, had he opened the card in her presence or allowed her to open it, she would probably have thought nothing of it. Briefly it occurred to her to wonder if he was testing her, trying to find out how much of a nuisance or how oppressive her love was going to prove to be.

'Can you blame me, Blythe?' Christian asked brutally.

'No.' She lifted unhappy eyes to his. 'I'm sorry, Christian. I know... I am trying.'

He shook his head dismissively as if he doubted her ability to succeed and indicated the cards and letters in front of her, the dissatisfied expression in his eyes tearing at her heart.

She started opening the mail, relaxing a little as she grew interested, questioning him about the identities of the people who had written, laughing at some of the messages.

'You really do know an incredible number of people,' she remarked again after a while.

'All with one thing in common at present,' Christian laughed. 'They can't wait to meet the lady who finally caught me.'

'Trapped you,' she corrected him softly.

'I walked in willingly, Blythe. You know that.' His lips twisted. 'At one stage I imagined I was trapping you.'

'When you thought I was marrying you out of obstinacy, refusing to back down after you'd called my bluff?'

'I never imagined that was the whole story,' he informed her drily. 'I thought it was allied to an adventurous inclination to indulge a taste for the novel and amusing.'

That had been while he'd still believed that her feelings for him matched the purely physical desire he felt for her.

'But now you know better,' she allowed flatly.

'Yes.' He spoke curtly.

'And it oppresses you,' she acknowledged mockingly.

'You know how it makes me feel.' He was dismissive.

Only in bed did his resentment fade, probably because in the grip of passion he could forget all the unwanted emotion she had brought to their marriage, aware only of her desire and his, for the hours that it ruled them.

With rare awkwardness, Blythe changed the subject. 'Most of the cards and letters are from England. How much longer are we going to be in Hong Kong?'

'I'm not sure.' Christian spoke with an odd reluctance. 'Originally I intended to be back in the UK by Christmas. Why?'

'And your house in England is going to be our permanent base, more or less, isn't it?' She smiled, hiding the perplexity his manner had occasioned. 'I must make arrangements for the contents of my simplex. I'll probably sell a lot of the furniture as you must have plenty, but there are one or two pieces I'd like to keep, and then there are my teddy-bears and pictures. I promise not to strew them all over your house, Christian, but I'd like a place for them, and I don't want to leave them in this house if we're going to spend most of our time in England. I'll find out about carriers. Then when I've disposed of everything, I can give up the simplex. I think my lease agreement stipulated more than a month's notice, so I'll have to surrender my deposit.'

'Don't do anything yet, Blythe.' The light blue eyes were wary.

'Why not?'

'It might be a mistake to rush it.' He paused and seemed to lose patience with his own caution, adding angrily, 'You might find yourself wishing you still had the simplex.'

A chill was creeping into her heart, but she made herself sound lightly teasing. 'Christian, our marriage isn't quite two weeks old! Isn't it a little premature to be deciding that it's a failure?'

'I'm not deciding anything.' His quick temper had risen, making his eyes blaze, and his voice was hard. 'But it might be the conclusion to which you yourself come in the fairly near future. Damn it, despite what we said just now, we don't really have a lot going for us. We had a kind of agreement not to let it matter while we were in Pattaya, and it didn't, but already the realities are creeping up on you, aren't they? I can't give you what you need, and you resent it. If it becomes an obsession it's going to either destroy you or you're going to save yourself by walking out, and, knowing you, I think it will be the latter. You believe in survival.'

'Then again, perhaps I'll find a way of dealing with it *and* staying in the marriage, Christian,' Blythe flared defiantly.

His temper seemed to subside as hers rose and he made a thoughtfully assessing examination of her creamy face, his eyes lingering on her tough little chin and generous mouth after dismissing the secretive eyes very quickly.

'You might, I suppose,' he conceded. 'But I can't help you, Blythe.'

It was something she would never get used to, the pain of hearing him say aloud and almost regretfully things she already knew. It hurt as much now as it had on their wedding night when he had admitted that he couldn't give her what she wanted and needed from him.

It took her several seconds to look up and give him a provocatively melting smile.

'There's one area in which this marriage works for both of us, anyway.'

'And works very well.'

Christian reached out, touching her hand where it lay on the table, and when she moved her fingers, seeking his pulse, she found it racing as hers was, and their eyes met, glimmering with intimate, mutual knowledge and promises of delight, the physical joy they found in each other unfailing.

So it was an unparalleled shock to Blythe when Christian went to sleep without making love to her that night.

He had been lying beside her after joining her in the huge bed in the attractive master bedroom, idly stroking her shoulder and the upper swell of one breast. Blythe's body was stirring languidly, her thighs slack with desire, but she was free of any immediate impatience these days, having learnt that the real ecstasy always came eventually, the culmination to other previously unimaginable delights.

She smiled confidently at him, and he moved his head, kissing her quickly and lightly on the mouth. Then he withdrew from her, put out the light and lay there.

Blythe was still and silent for a long time, but finally she had to ask.

'Is this usual?' she enquired, voice almost a whisper.

'It's all right, don't worry about it.' His voice was indulgent, but remote at the same time.

'I don't know these things, you see,' she added tartly.

'No, you don't, do you?' Abruptly his tone assumed a bitter ring that appalled her. 'You'll learn. Goodnight, sleep well.'

But Blythe couldn't sleep. For a while she sensed that he too was awake, but eventually the rhythm of his breathing changed as he drifted off.

Her eyes burned and her heart was tightly encased in anguish. She thought she knew what Christian was trying to do. Having embarked on marriage so heedlessly, thinking it would be an amusing adventure, and then finding himself with a wife who loved him, he was probably prepared to accept that he was partly responsible for the mess and wait for her to be the one to end it. But he was naturally impatient, and being loved made him uncomfortable.

So he was trying to hasten her departure, to drive her away from him. He knew—he had mentioned it more than once—that the one area in which his feelings equalled hers was in bed. He did not fail her there, his need and the satisfaction he found in her body the match of hers.

Now he had decided to start failing her. If he gave her nothing, in any area, he had probably reasoned, the lack would speed her on her way.

Blythe did not believe he had stopped wanting her, and she knew what she had to do. She had to suppress anything which would keep him aware of her love. It was that, the emotion, which offended him.

So she would hide it from now on, she decided resolutely, confident that she could do it because so much was at stake.

When she awoke in the pearly dawn, Christian was already awake, watching her broodingly, his dark early-morning beard adding to the moodiness of his expression.

Smiling, last night's resolve vivid in her mind, Blythe stretched luxuriously, deliberately bringing her body into contact with his and feeling his instantaneous response.

'I was afraid I'd worn you out,' she murmured wickedly.

'No, Blythe, I don't think you'll ever do that. Damn you, I think I'm always going to want you,' he predicted, harsh with resentment.

It hurt to hear it, but at the same time she felt a surge of bitter triumph. She did have this to build on.

Christian's mouth, hands and body were hard and urgent. He entered her swiftly, filling her with sharp, powerful thrusts yet somehow retaining sufficient control over the intensity of his desire to be able to wait until she was bucking beneath him, choked cries of pleasure rising from her, before surrendering with a stifled groan to the devastation of his own shattering climax.

Bodies slick with sweat, they collapsed together, and it was a long time before Christian could raise his head to look into Blythe's face.

'If that's what a night's abstinence does, I don't think I'll try it again,' he murmured, the hand that stroked her arm trembling slightly.

'Oh, I don't know. It was...exciting,' Blythe confided languidly, and held up a hand for him to see. 'Look—I'm still shaking too.'

Christian laughed softly. 'You're incorrigible!'

'Insatiable,' she corrected him naughtily, then sobered. 'It's always different, every time. How many ways are there, Christian?'

'As many as we want there to be.'

And she would use them all, she promised herself, because Christian's desire for her was all she had to work with, and what would she do if one day it stopped renewing itself?

'And it goes on,' she murmured, an optimistic superstition suggesting that stating it aloud would make it true. 'Forever.'

'But how long will it be enough for you, without the rest, the absolutes you need? No, don't answer,' Christian stopped her as she tensed in response to the brooding question. 'I know you now, I think. For now, you'll try to make it enough, won't you?'

'Yes!' She was emphatic.

'You've got bottle,' he commented unexpectedly, and smiled. 'Shall we take the morning off?'

'You've got all those meetings set up,' Blythe reminded him regretfully. 'And as you said my presence wouldn't be necessary, I'm going to extend my lunch hour and go shopping in Nathan Road.'

It was an impulsive decision. She would buy something seductive and wear it to bed that night. She was going to turn herself into the ultimate vamp in order to keep this frail marriage of theirs alive for as long as possible, she promised herself, ignoring the vague feeling of distaste the idea engendered.

She came to her senses in Nathan Road several hours later. The black lace she had been envisaging would turn her into a caricature. She could only be what she was and no more. It had been enough to make Christian want her in the first place, so she must hope and pray that it was enough to keep his interest in her and their marriage alive. If it palled——

Blythe shivered. Then he would look for someone new. You couldn't impose fidelity. Only love did that, because it was love's natural choice.

There was only one other thing she could do to aid her own cause, and that meant adhering to last night's resolve, as Christian hated reminders of her unwanted love. Quite apart from her own interests, she owed him

that, she realised guiltily. She had been wrong to marry
him, loving him and knowing his distaste for the
emotion.

Her resolve was tested almost immediately. As she
glanced into a new restaurant to see if it looked the sort
of establishment at which she could buy a carton of
yoghurt to take away for her lunch, and dismissed it as
far too exclusive, her attention was arrested by a couple
seated at one of the tables, a waiter hovering deferen-
tially close by.

Her husband was lunching with Trish Crewe. Just the
two of them. No Rollo to render the assignation
innocent.

Anger came before pain. Blythe's eyes blazed and she
took a step towards the restaurant's entrance, intent on
externalising the emotion suddenly boiling within her.
She would tear Christian away from that woman, inflict
violence on both of them, shout her rage and inchoate
agony——

And lose Christian forever, she realised, granted the
mercy of a second's sanity.

Her small face growing bleak, she stared at them.
Christian had his jacket off, while Trish wore a white
blouse with a black bow beneath a waistcoat in a
Christmassy-looking but perhaps legitimate tartan, red
and green with a black stripe.

Blythe turned away just as Christian was raising his
head to consult the waiter, so she didn't know if he had
seen her or not, but the merest glimpse of her departing
figure would have been enough, she supposed, since he
had commented on her outfit that morning and it was
one of her most boldly distinctive, big white polka-dots
on a soft crimson background.

She abandoned all thought of returning to the office,
knowing that if Christian followed her too soon she

would not yet have succeeded in gathering sufficient self-control to dam her rage and bitter hurt. They would come pouring out; she would make a scene, as Vicky Short had once done, and confirm Christian forever in his belief that inexperienced women who fell in love with him were to be avoided.

She and Christian had travelled to the office in the Rolls that morning, so it required the subway, the tram up to the Peak and her own feet to get her home.

Only when she was safely there did Blythe yield to the tears that had been threatening all the way, a brief storm of anger, fear and sheer unhappiness, to which guilt presently added itself because she knew she had had no right to marry a man like Christian without first warning him that she loved him. By doing so, she had turned him into a cheat.

But she wouldn't let him go. She couldn't! Eyes dry once more, she cleansed her face and re-did her subtle make-up, thinking about it, remembering her earlier resolve. Whether he had seen her staring at him and Trish or not, she wasn't going to mention it—or mention other women at all, either specifically or generally. That way the resentment he felt might at least remain contained, and if it wasn't enough to guarantee the success of their marriage, at least she need not lose him quite yet.

But she needed time to school herself. Belatedly responsible, she rang Triple A and suffered anew when she learned that Christian was still absent, visualising him still with Trish, but no longer at the restaurant. They had gone elsewhere——

Abruptly she left a message for him, explaining that she had gone home, and rang off.

The ache in her heart was a living, burning torment. *Was* Christian still with Trish?

If Christian had only loved her——

But he didn't. Blythe didn't believe he would go so far as to extend his betrayal to the point of actual infidelity just yet, with their marriage only approximately two weeks old and in view of the way he had made love to her that morning, but the probable truth was almost as unpalatable as that would have been. It had been the refreshment of Trish's company that he had sought. Trish didn't love him.

All the same, she wished she knew the average length of his various affairs. Then she would have some idea of when to expect him to grow bored with her body.

Christian wore his new, heartbreakingly reserved expression when he came home, walking into the lounge where she had arranged herself languidly on the couch after observing his arrival from the window.

'Are you all right?' he enquired neutrally, shrugging out of his jacket and tossing it on to a chair.

Blythe's hand strayed in the direction of the jade Buddha on the table beside her, but she crushed the impulse, remembering the private promises she had made to herself.

'Yes, now. I'm sorry about my absence this afternoon. Did you get my message? I had a headache,' she lied, observing him from beneath half-closed lids and shaping a witty smile. 'Perhaps we should blame this morning's somewhat violent activity!'

'You always seek refuge in sex, don't you?' Christian was loosening his tie. 'Allusions to it, anyway, if not the act.'

'Well, it does rather dominate our lives just now,' she reasoned smartly, the words too quick and a little breathless as he strolled towards her.

He crouched beside her, hard fingers capturing her chin as she looked away from him.

'You should have slapped on a damn sight more make-up if you wanted me to believe you. Or do headaches always reduce you to tears?' His hard, intent gaze rested on the faint redness around her eyes. 'Did you think I hadn't seen you?'

'I wasn't sure,' she admitted tautly, lowering her eyes again as he released her and straightened up. 'Just remember that you raised the subject, Christian. I wasn't going to mention it.'

'But it would have been there, wouldn't it?' He turned away, then swung round to face her again. 'How long are you going to subject yourself to this, Blythe? *This time* I'll give you an explanation. You'd already disappeared on your shopping expedition when I got back to the office and Trish called, wanting to have lunch. The object was money—my money, some of which she needs if she's going to lobby various organisations and political bodies on behalf of a couple of refugee families whose cause she's taken up and who are in danger of repatriation.'

'I suppose she got it?' Blythe hated to hear herself.

'Yes. The circumstances are exceptional and urgent,' Christian added curtly. 'There's only one other thing I'm prepared to tell you, and I should probably have done so long ago, but, as you said when I discovered the facts of your relationship with Captain Smith, we were playing games, fostering each other's illusions, trying to pique each other's interest, curiosity, jealousy...whatever. Trish and I were never lovers.'

Outrage swamped caution. 'Do you have to lie as well as everything else?' she demanded. 'You dumped Vicky Short for her.'

'Trish kindly supplied me with a reason for dumping Vicky, if that's what you insist on believing I did.' Christian's temper rose. 'Yes, I know I made a mess of it. I was mildly interested in Vicky, although I wasn't even thinking in terms of an actual affair, just a flirtation, the sort of thing which would provide me with company, someone to go out and about with while I was here. Then I realised that she was a total innocent who imagined she was in love with me. I didn't want to get into that sort of scene, but for some reason I thought I needed a more substantial excuse for cooling it. Trish agreed to play along... I was stupid. I thought Vicky would make a dignified retreat, but it didn't work that way.'

'Because she was an innocent.' Blythe was scathing. 'She might not have stayed that way if you'd indulged your mild interest, Christian. *I'm* not a virgin any longer.'

'No, but I'm still the only lover you've ever had and am likely to remain so for years to come. Do you know what a burden that is to me? How it makes me feel?' He couldn't conceal his resentment. 'But we're straying from the point. What's all this doing to you, Blythe? What are you doing to yourself? Look at you! You're losing your lovely sense of humour, for a start... Will it always be this way? Trish wasn't my lover, I've never wanted her to be, whether you accept it or not, but it's not unlikely that at some stage in the future I, or both of us together, will meet up with someone who *has* been my lover in the past, although I've had nowhere near as many affairs as you persist in imagining—lord, I'd have to have been incredibly irresponsible in all sorts of ways! But what then? Do we go through all this again? And again?'

'How many agains are there likely to be, precisely? I'd like to know in advance,' Blythe averred waspishly, saw the anger blaze in Christian's face and held up a pacifying hand. 'I know, I know. But it's you who's doing this! You raised the subject, you're the one who's so defensive, not to mention resentful. Oh, why don't you just turn me out now? Ask me to leave?'

'No, I don't think I'll ever do that.' As his anger subsided, Christian's expression became closed and unreadable. 'But it's a decision you may take for yourself, when you realise how much of your essential self is being lost, or subdued by your awareness that I couldn't bring to our marriage what you brought, and heaven knows it haunts me probably even more than it does you; you'll lose that intrinsic lightness of spirit that attracts so magically, everything, and I'll be responsible... When it becomes too much, I won't stop you. Remember that. You're free to go any time.'

He probably hoped she would do so at once, Blythe reflected bitterly.

'I won't—I can't! You must know that, Christian. You know how I feel about you,' she reminded him chokingly. 'I worship you!'

Abruptly he seated himself beside her on the couch, putting an arm round her shoulders.

'And I don't deserve it,' he acknowledged sombrely. 'I don't deserve you because I can't... I can't give you guarantees that mean anything. My past invalidates anything I might say.'

'If you stopped saying it, if you stopped reminding me...' she faltered. 'If we could pretend... it might be easier?'

Christian looked dubious, but he said flatly, 'If that's what you want?'

'Please,' she requested him achingly, letting him see her eyes, and he seemed to wince a little in response to the rare humility she evinced.

'We can try,' was all he could offer, bending his head to kiss her soft, shining curls before changing the subject. 'What do you want to do tonight, go out or stay here?'

'I was going to make you a stir-fry,' Blythe remembered.

It seemed an age since she had planned it, in another, happier time, before she had seen him with Trish.

'I'll help you,' he volunteered. 'But first I want a drink and a shower. Let me get you something too. Perrier?'

'Please.' Making an effort, she gave him a quick, teasing smile. 'It still surprises me, the interest you take in helping or watching me in the kitchen. It doesn't go with the playboy image.'

He ignored that. 'Why shouldn't I admire excellence, when my own skills there are basic, if adequate? It intrigues me to see someone who takes real pride and pleasure in the creation of meals, although you still haven't been able to explain satisfactorily just why you enjoy it so much.'

'I don't know. It's just . . . fulfilling.'

The subject of his lunch with Trish was closed, and never re-opened in the days that followed.

Those days became weeks, and Blythe was conscious that they were both making an effort to ignore the things that flawed their marriage, Christian's inability to love and the varied history that guaranteed that one day, sooner or later, he was going to tire of her and want someone new, if not in his bed then facing him across a restaurant table, or beside him somewhere else, or in his arms on some dance-floor.

'There are things we're avoiding talking about, aren't there?' she couldn't help prompting one evening.

'I thought you wanted it that way?'

'Yes.'

'Then don't rock the boat,' he advised.

'But it's always there, all the time,' she protested. 'Except perhaps in bed.'

There, everything else, including fear, was lost in the triumph of knowing that here at least he needed her for now, and that she was capable of satisfying him in the most earth-shaking way.

'There's no room for anything else in bed,' Christian agreed, eyes glinting. 'Your energy and inventiveness are a delight, over and over again.'

'You're pretty imaginative yourself,' Blythe retorted happily.

'Are you ever happy at other times as well?' he asked her unexpectedly.

'Oh, yes,' she assured him.

It was true. She could be happy, answering his challenges at work, lying beside him on the beach at Repulse Bay, or wandering around Hong Kong's renowned night market, clinging to his hand for fear of losing him in the crowd.

But the question always returned to haunt her. How long would she have him?

If he couldn't love her, then there was no way in which she could bind him to her. But the temptation was always there. She would find herself contemplating other ways— cheating ways, she always realised, ashamed.

She even considered allowing herself to become pregnant, and was horrified a moment later. Dear heaven, hadn't she selfishly done enough damage simply by loving him and marrying him? To take a unilateral decision to create what would in essence be a permanent, perpetual link between them, outlasting even their marriage, would not only be unforgivable but would consolidate the resentment Christian already felt.

Loving him really had turned her into a cheat if she could even consider such a thing. A shaky marriage was the last reason in the world for having a child, even if it was a mutual decision; no one had the right to impose the burden of mending adult messes on a tiny innocent.

Blythe knew she could only go on trying to make the most of her marriage while it lasted.

CHAPTER TEN

IT HAD to happen eventually.

Blythe found herself face to face with Vicky Short in a descending lift.

His assessment of Triple A itself completed, Christian was still intent on gauging the mood of Hong Kong's business community before coming to a final decision as to whether to relocate the airline's headquarters.

He had gone out that afternoon to solicit the views of a banker who had already made a firm decision to stay and face 1997 and, calling to take Blythe home at the end of the day, he had merely rung through from the ground floor to say he was waiting for her, so she was alone when the encounter with Vicky took place.

'Hello,' Blythe murmured neutrally, and turned her attention to the lights above the lift door as it slid closed, deciding that in Vicky's place she wouldn't want to make trivial conversation.

No token greeting came in response, and after a few seconds Blythe found the silence disconcerting. She stared at the lights, willing the lift to hurry, but it was a notoriously slow one, usually avoided, so it was also unlikely that they would stop to take in anyone else on the way down.

Then Vicky said abruptly, 'I suppose you're feeling very pleased with yourself?'

Blythe glanced at her. She was a slender, willowy girl, taller than she was, with baby-blonde hair worn in a deep fringe, and her lovely violet eyes were huge and hurt.

'Excuse me?' Blythe asked blankly, to give her the chance to regret whatever impulse had prompted her and retreat without too much damage.

'I said you must be very pleased with yourself.' The silvery voice was somehow malevolent. 'Because Christian Ballantine actually went as far as marrying you. Well, I suppose someone like you knows how to hold on to a man——'

'Don't do this,' Blythe interrupted gently.

'Why not? It can't hurt. People like you and Christian Ballantine don't get hurt, and you don't care about those of us who do.' Vicky's eyes were filling. 'You're two of a kind, I'm sure, but I wonder if even you can hold on to him forever.'

'That's my problem, not yours,' Blythe asserted evenly.

'In a way, I almost wish you would,' Vicky went on. 'I wish you'd keep him chained to you forever, and that he'd hate it—he would hate it eventually, because he'll never be satisfied with just one woman.'

'You're embarrassing me.' Blythe sighed. 'And you'll probably be even more embarrassed yourself when you've got over this. Stop it, Vicky. I'm sorry you were hurt, but I wasn't responsible. I didn't even work for Triple A at the time.'

'Trish Biddulph wasn't really responsible either. He was—Christian Ballantine.' Vicky's mouth was working. 'He uses women and discards them. Or he flirts with them, leading them on, then drops them flat when someone more attractive comes along.'

'You were probably lucky.' Blythe was aware that it was unkind and tactless, but she believed it was true. 'You're not . . . tough enough for Christian.'

Vicky was still a baby emotionally, she reflected, glancing at her again, and she would probably always be, however much experience she might acquire. Everything about her proclaimed her a victim, one of those unhappy women who got hurt over and over again, never learning, letting men use them, idealistically believing that this time, this man was different.

Except that Christian hadn't used her. He hadn't been the one to initiate the awful cycle.

'Whereas you are,' Vicky was suggesting. 'Oh, I don't suppose you'll ever suffer much. For all I know, you've agreed to an open marriage anyway. You and Christian are that sort of people. You make a mockery of love. I'm sure you went into your marriage with your eyes wide open... But do you know what your husband did to me——?'

'Vicky, let it go,' Blythe urged quickly.

The lights above them indicated that they were about to reach the ground floor. A knot of tension had formed in her stomach and she could only view the prospect with relief, but she wanted to spare the other girl the humiliation of having her distress witnessed by whoever happened to be in the normally crowded concourse when the door slid open.

'He was interested in me. I fell in love with him and he let me believe there was going to be something between us. He took me out, he touched me... He even broke off his relationship with a woman in England. I know because I heard him telephone her and say she shouldn't wait for him, and after that he was even more obvious, so I let him see how I felt. Then he decided he preferred Trish Biddulph... And that's the way it's going to be all his life. There'll always be someone new, someone he prefers——'

Blythe heard no more. The door had opened and Christian was standing there in front of the row of lifts, chatting to the head of the personnel department while he waited for Blythe.

'What's wrong?' he asked sharply, noticing her pallor as she emerged and he stepped forward to meet her.

'Nothing. Let's go,' Blythe said tightly, giving the head of Personnel a strained smile.

'Are——' Christian broke off as Vicky rushed past them, gulping audibly. 'That's——'

'Never mind! Come on,' urged Blythe, taking his arm and shaking it a little. 'Where are you parked? In your underground bay?'

With a look of silent comprehension he accompanied her into the separate lift that serviced the building's covered parking.

'What's she been saying to you?' he demanded as they descended.

'Nothing I didn't already know,' Blythe snapped, following it with an irritable movement. 'You'd think she'd have learnt her lesson after her last famous scene, wouldn't you?'

'Blythe——'

'I don't want to discuss it,' she added imperiously, knowing what would happen if they did.

'I think we'll have to,' he said quietly. 'But it can wait.'

There was a cynically brooding darkness to Christian's face and his mouth assumed a moody shape as he drove them to the house on the Peak, speaking only occasionally and then solely of matters pertaining to Triple A.

It suited Blythe, grappling with fear and uncertainty.

In the end Vicky had got to her. Yes, there would always be someone new, someone Christian preferred, as that woman Vicky said he had telephoned must once have been preferred to whoever there had been before her, and as Vicky, for a time, had been preferred to her.

She understood why he had needed to hurt Vicky, but it didn't change anything else. One day she too was going to lose him as all the others before had done. The fact that she was his wife might make it slightly more difficult for him to move on, but that was all.

When they got home, Christian went out to the patio since the afternoon's rain was over, the sun shining. He always preferred to have a drink before showering and changing, while Blythe reversed the ritual.

His face was still darkly unreadable when she joined him, soft apricot harem-style pants whispering sensuously about her legs, and she felt that remoteness as a rejection, her heart clenching.

Christian turned his head to look at her as she sat down with her glass of Perrier, and apprehension became terror as for once he ignored her clothes, despite the temptation offered by her alluring little top, designed to be both revealing and mysteriously concealing.

'You look pale,' he commented expressionlessly.

'I'm frightened,' she said simply. 'Christian, I haven't said a word, so why... You can't... Please——'

'Stop it, Blythe!' His lips twisted with disgust. 'Don't do that to yourself. I can't stand it! I want to know what Vicky Short said to you.'

'Nothing much. She just told me what had happened between you, which I already knew.' Blythe sent him an oblique look. 'Why do we have to discuss it? I understand why you had to reject her.'

'Do you?' The distant tone was wounding.

'Oh, yes.' She risked a challenging little smile. 'You were being cruel to be kind, because she'd fallen in love with you and you had nothing to give her in return. It would have been worse, ultimately, if you hadn't rejected her. She'd have been hurt far more badly, and she's not a very controlled person. Maybe one day she'll realise what you did, when other men have hurt her in other worse ways, as I'm afraid they will... You decided not to be one of them.'

'I botched it, though, didn't I?' he prompted grimly.

'You just didn't realise soon enough.' A mistake she had helped him repeat with her, Blythe reflected, and laughed forlornly. 'You're attractive to women, Christian. You can't expect to get it right every time, with the numbers of women who must fall in love with you, or even just want you.'

'You do,' he asserted surprisingly, his gaze grown reluctantly curious. 'You also attract, but it hasn't seemed to burden you. Quite apart from the fact that you were untouched when you married me, there's no hint of a trail of broken-hearted or frustrated men in your wake. Have you never hurt anyone?'

The change of subject relieved her and she took it up swiftly, despite a certain sensitivity.

'There was a boy once when I was sixteen. All the girls were after him, but he wanted me. I'd only just discovered how boys looked at me, so I suppose I...flirted. He was one of those boys with all-round star quality, handsome, macho, good at sport and academically gifted, but I didn't love him, so I couldn't... He cried.' Shame had hushed her voice. 'I was horrified, appalled, and I promised I'd never do that to anyone again. I learnt to deal with what I was and accept the responsibility, in not such a very different way from you, except that you did allow yourself a sex life. I couldn't. I've always made sure that people—men—knew from the start where they stood and where it stopped if I didn't love them. It's kinder.'

'You are kind.' Christian shook his head with a faint sigh. 'Seven years younger than me, but a whole lot kinder and wiser. And look at you now. You deserve better than this, Blythe. Why don't you get out?'

She was silent for a while, absorbing the pain, adjusting to it.

'Do you want me to?' she finally asked numbly.

'I think so. Yes, I do,' Christian added more emphatically.

'But you're not tired of me yet.' Blythe raised furiously glittering eyes to his face for a moment. 'Last night when I kissed you when you weren't expecting it and you nearly cracked my ribs hugging me, you said I was in your blood . . . And I know what happens to your body when we touch, Christian, and that we can make love all night and you'll still——'

'Damn it, Blythe, this has nothing to do with sex!' Christian interrupted tempestuously, his glass making a cracking sound as he set it on the table beside hers. 'It's the way you feel, and what it's doing to you. I can't bear seeing it, it's doing something terrible to you, destroying you. Oh, you haven't wanted to make an issue of what Vicky Short said to you, but you were thinking about it all the way home, weren't you? About all the women there've been in my life, wondering who and how many would come after you, and when . . . You were suffering, torturing yourself, and there's nothing I can do to help you. You're trying so hard, but it's not working, because even if it's not coming out, it's still there inside you, which is probably worse.'

'I can handle it. You don't have to feel guilty,' Blythe flared defiantly, and gave him a brittle smile. 'I expect there are ways you could force me to go, but I'm not voluntarily walking out of this marriage until you get tired of me, Christian.'

'So will you hang in there, fighting, to the bitter end?' Christian's exasperation was touched with wry, amused resignation. 'And I'm so afraid it will be very bitter, my darling—unbearably so.'

'It's hardly a life sentence,' she retorted in a falsely consoling tone. 'Don't worry, you'll get tired of me— you know that. It will probably even happen quite soon.'

'How can it?' he demanded harshly. 'My God, if it were just lust, then yes! I could control it, cool it, turn it off. But when it's not just my loins that are involved here, but my heart, my head, everything . . . How can I ever tire of you, Blythe?'

'Your heart?' she asked sharply.

'You know that.'

She hit him hard, her open hand striking his jaw. 'Your heart!'

'What was that for?' Christian was regarding her as if she had gone utterly mad.

Perhaps she had. She was on her feet, grasping him by the shoulders and trying to shake him.

'Your heart!' she choked again.

'Didn't you know?' Christian was incredulous.

'How? You never said! But . . .'

Sudden doubt assailed her, dissolving her anger, and he was able to draw her downwards until she was kneeling on the patio before him, trapped between his knees.

'Not an appropriate position,' he murmured drily. 'I should be the one kneeling before you. What the hell is this all about, Blythe?'

Hardly able to breathe for fear and hope, she looked up at him, her eyes dark with the two emotions.

'You said... Oh, you've said it over and over again, Christian!' she protested brokenly. 'You've said you couldn't give me what I need and want from you, and heaven knows I've felt your resentment ever since you found out that I'd never had any lovers.'

'Of course I've felt resentment, and so much of it!' he agreed tautly, and fear rose while hope sank, and with it her heart. 'I've felt resentful of you for coming to our marriage with no previous lovers in your past—and resentful too of my own past. No, I can't give you what you need, the proof that I'll be faithful, when I have a few lovers in *my* past, although nowhere near as many as you and popular opinion seem to believe. My history counters any promises I might make. Only time can convince you, but you'll destroy yourself with fear and suspicion in that time. You can't trust me, and there's no way that I can prove to you that you can. I can't give you that peace of mind, I can't give you that security, and I hate myself for it. Sometimes, lord forgive me, I feel as if I hate you too—and there's a bloody irony. Before we were married I used to keep raising the subject of your supposed lovers, taunting you, half in the hope that you'd deny them, because I wanted to be first, only, most important. Oh, yes, the great double standard. Then, when I knew there hadn't been any, I wished there'd been scores, so that I needn't feel so guilty, as if I'd entered our marriage somehow... spoilt for you. When I realised why you'd married me, the joy was cancelled by my simultaneous realisation of your expectations, your rights, your need to be able to trust me, and I couldn't give you that. I failed you... I felt, and feel, so unworthy, so undeserving!'

'But...' Blythe hesitated, then took the risk and went for the gap. 'Christian, do you love me?'

'Of course.' He was impatiently dismissive of the obvious. 'Blythe——'

Fingers biting into his shoulders halted him.

'Just a moment. Do you think you could bear to pause a while in inviting me to leave you and tell me about it?' she requested, her voice silky-soft with the rage that gripped her again. 'About loving me, Christian?'

'What is there to tell?' He looked at her as if she were stupid, then gave in with a savagely reminiscent laugh. 'I loved you the moment I saw you, when Lau introduced us. I didn't expect it and didn't particularly want it, but there it was. I resented it, then resented you for being what I thought you were...that double standard again. But there was nothing I could do. I did try to resist it for a few hours, I suppose. Then you were kind...you were concerned that I might not know about Trish's marriage and be hurt by it. I was lost forever then. Kindness as well as everything else was too much... Only, despite the kindness, you didn't seem to like me much... So we played our games, and by the time you tried to send me fleeing in terror by raising the idea of marriage I thought I knew you well enough to be sure that you wouldn't back down easily if I called your bluff, and by that stage I was desperate enough to want you on any terms... What did you say?'

'I said—likewise!' Blythe told him tautly.

'I also thought that being married to you would give me an advantage over all the other men I imagined you'd known but who hadn't been married to you,' he went on, agitated now.

'Again, likewise,' she muttered. 'That's what I thought about myself and the other women in your life.'

'I wanted you for all time, for life,' Christian added, his pupils dilating with emotion as he stared at her.

'That's why I didn't try to make love to you during our brief engagement. I was afraid that once we became lovers you might back out, decide marriage wasn't necessary... Because I didn't know then why you were marrying me, Blythe. I thought it was for the novelty, the adventure. I knew you seemed resentful of the other women I'd been involved with, but it didn't worry me to any great extent because I thought if it got too bad I could point out that you were being unreasonable when I accepted the men in your past, although heaven knows the thought of them seared me with jealousy, but I wasn't going to let you know that. Then, when we were married and I realised that there hadn't been any men... The gift you gave me assured me of your love and fidelity, and I couldn't give you any similar assurance in return. I did resent you, Blythe, however unreasonably, but most of all I wished I could have come to our marriage as innocent as you. I regretted everything in my past, however enjoyable, because I knew it increased your insecurity. I wished... Oh, God, I wished I could have been a virgin for you as you were for me, so that we were starting out together and equal, and you could be as sure of me as I was of you.'

'Why don't we just say you were practising to be ready for me even if you didn't realise it?' Blythe suggested shakily.

Then, abruptly, she was weeping wildly as Christian's arms came round her.

'What have I done now?' His face was white and shocked as she drew back to look at him through the dazzle of her tears. 'Oh, darling, don't! I know how unhappy you are, unable to trust me. That's why I think——'

'You stupid, stupid fool of a man,' she sobbed, but a laugh broke through as well. 'If you'd told me! It was all you had to do, and none of this would have been necessary.'

Christian closed his eyes for a moment, but they were still appalled when he opened them.

'Is that what you needed? All you needed?'

'That's all. To know.'

'My heart, what have I done to you?' He waited, cradling her in his arms, until both her tears and the odd half relieved, half incredulous little laugh had ceased. 'I have no excuse. Initially a sort of pride kept me silent because I didn't think you loved me. Then I asked you if you knew why I'd married you and you said yes, so I did think you knew then. I didn't quite know how to put it into words, but I thought I was showing you. I'm a novice at loving. I've never loved anyone before... Never loved a woman, I mean. When I was growing up, I loved my parents, of course. They knew I did and I knew they loved me, but we never said so. In our family, you didn't express deep emotion in words——'

'Could you try now?' she ventured lovingly. 'Just once, Christian. You'll never have to do it again, because I'll remember. Then the other women in your past won't matter, because I'll know there aren't going to be any in the future... only me.'

'Only you, always, Blythe.' His lips brushed the curve of her throat. 'I love you. Why only once?'

'As many times as you like,' she invited him joyously, her arms about him. 'But save some breath for other things... although I suppose this is even earlier than we went to bed on our wedding night.'

Christian's laughter was a little shaken as her hands began travelling. 'And there I was thinking we could take a drive down to your simplex and pick up all your teddy-bears, because once they move in I'll know I've got you for all time.'

'I think we could negotiate a compromise, don't you?' Blythe kissed him happily, then gasped as his fingers skimmed one swelling breast. 'We've got all night, and tomorrow isn't a working day, so we can fit everything in, bed and teddy-bears and food and champagne, and bed... Christian, I love you quite desperately!'

He couldn't answer, and for the first time Blythe, feeling him tremble in her arms, knew that he did so in love as well as desire.

Many hours later, the house on the Peak stood silent and in darkness.

'Wake up, Christian,' Blythe said to her husband, wriggling in his arms. 'I need to ask you something.'

'Don't tell me you've stopped trusting me already,' he mumbled into the warm curve of her neck.

'I'll trust you forever,' she whispered.

'Because that's how long I'll love you,' he agreed. 'What is it?'

'I forgot to ask you...' Her concentration lapsed for a moment as he moved against her, and kept lapsing as she tried to continue, 'Do you think that... perhaps not immediately, but in a year or two...we could...Christian, let me finish!'

'Have a baby,' he finished for her, raising himself on one elbow. 'Do you want one?'

'I want your baby.' Blythe's lips parted against his warm flesh.

'I want yours.'

'Ours.' There was a pause. 'It would please your parents.'

Christian laughed softly. 'It would please me, and if it pleases you, my darling Blythe . . . then as many babies as you like!'

'Oh! Now, just a minute, Christian!'

'You've never said that before.'

'I meant about the babies . . . Oh, I can't think . . .'

'You're not supposed to. This isn't an intellectual exercise.'

'A loving one,' she whispered.

'Always that, Blythe,' Christian confirmed, and she had no more to say just then.

The laughter was back and the loving had always been there. It always would be.

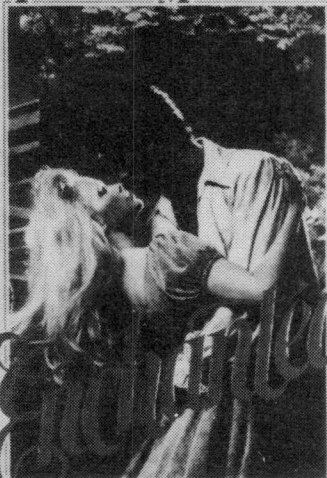

An irresistible offer from Mills & Boon

Here's a personal invitation from Mills & Boon Reader Service, to become a regular reader of Romances. To welcome you, we'd like you to have 4 books, a CUDDLY TEDDY and a special MYSTERY GIFT absolutely FREE.

Then you could look forward each month to receiving 6 brand new Romances, delivered to your door, postage and packing free! Plus our free newsletter featuring author news, competitions, special offers and much more.

This invitation comes with no strings attached. You may cancel or suspend your subscription at any time, and still keep your free books and gifts.

It's so easy. Send no money now. Simply fill in the coupon below and post it to -
Reader Service, FREEPOST, PO Box 236, Croydon, Surrey CR9 9EL.

--------------------------------- NO STAMP REQUIRED ---------------------------------

Free Books Coupon

Yes! Please rush me my 4 free Romances and 2 free gifts! Please also reserve me a Reader Service subscription. If I decide to subscribe I can look forward to receiving 6 brand new Romances each month for just £9.60, postage and packing free. If I choose not to subscribe I shall write to you within 10 days - I can keep the books and gifts whatever I decide. I may cancel or suspend my subscription at any time. I am over 18 years of age.

Name Mrs/Miss/Ms/Mr _____ EP18R

Address _____

_____

Postcode_____ Signature _____

Mills & Boon

Forthcoming Titles

BEST SELLER ROMANCE
Available in February

DARKNESS INTO LIGHT Carole Mortimer
BLIND DATE Emma Darcy

COLLECTION
Available in February

The Betty Neels Collection
AT THE END OF THE DAY
NEVER THE TIME AND THE PLACE

The Patricia Wilson Collection
A MOMENT OF ANGER
BRIDE OF DIAZ

MEDICAL ROMANCE
Available in February

CAUGHT IN THE CROSSFIRE Sara Burton
PRACTICE MAKES PERFECT Caroline Anderson
WINGS OF HEALING Marion Lennox
YESTERDAY'S MEMORY Patricia Robertson